WICKED WOMEN

A N D   O T H E R   S T O R I E S

ALSO BY SALLY WALKER BRINKMANN

Rebel Traveler
Between River and Mountain (forthcoming)

WICKED WOMEN

A N D   O T H E R   S T O R I E S

SALLY WALKER BRINKMANN

WILDSIDE PRESS

CONTENTS

WICKED WOMEN

MORGAN COUNTY, WEST VIRGINIA

Molly Finch was watching TV late on Friday night. The 11:00 o'clock news had just begun when she heard the screeching of brakes. A delivery truck had stopped on the side of Route 522 in front of her house. In response to repeated banging on her front door, Molly found herself facing a tired-looking driver.

"You Molly Finch?" he asked.

"Yeah," she answered hesitantly through the cracked and chained door.

"Finch of Friendship Labs?" He shuffled log sheets.

"What? What the hell are you talking about? This ain't no lab. You've made a mistake," she snapped, but she patted her platinum blond hair in place. He wasn't a bad-looking kid.

The driver checked the address again. "No mistake, Ma'am. Look, I'm on a schedule. I'll just drop your order by the garage door. Please sign here."

"I ain't signing nothing." Molly's voice took on a shrill edge. "Get outta here."

"Look, Ma'am." He backed away. "I don't know what the problem is. This was a rush order. It cost extra but the order's paid for. It's yours, so I'm dumping it and leaving."

"You ain't dumping nothing," Molly shouted as the man hurried toward the truck. Fifteen minutes later, 20 containers of lab rats, squeaking and scrambling in their cages, were stacked on Molly's gravel driveway.

"Have a good day," the driver yelled over Molly's sobs and curses. He jumped into the truck and drove off.

Dumbfounded, Molly watched him drive away. She ran a small beauty shop in her home—not a laboratory. Finally, she got up the nerve to walk down to the pile of cages. She had never seen a rat up close before and now stared open-mouthed at hundreds of them. A sheaf of papers was clipped to the nearest cage. She forced herself to get close enough to grab it. Then she ran back into the house and bolted the door behind her. The statement read: "25 white rats, female. 200 white rats, male." She skipped through the rest of the bill to the bottom line. "Amount due: $625.00." Her credit card number was entered on the payment line.

How the hell could this have happened to her, and why? Then she saw the small card clipped to the bottom of the bill. Printed in large letters was this message. "When a friend is a rat, then rats will be her friends."

Still holding the papers, Molly sank down on the couch and cried, "Shit! That bitch, Juanita. This is all her doing. It's to do with her old man and me. Oh, shit!" Molly pounded the couch cushions with her small fists and started to bawl. "That sonuvabitch sure wasn't worth it," she sobbed.

* * * *

On the ridge road above Molly's house, an old black Bronco started up and moved slowly away. "Yes!" Dixie yelled. "We done stuck it to that grabby bitch, Molly. That'll be the last time she messes around with somebody else's man."

Amid the laughter and cheering, Juanita poured out paper cups of champagne and passed them to the other women. "Yeah, I'd have loved to see the look on her face. Matter a fact, she's welcome to that bastard. And, Sylvia, I have you to thank. Your cousin at the lab got the timing perfect. Molly's gonna be stuck with the shipment until morning."

"She's gonna haveta spend the night with the rats—perfect!" Dixie whooped, banging on the side of the car through the open window and yelled, "Sweet dreams, Friendship Lab."

Sylvia pulled the car off the road. "I propose a toast. To us. To the women." She drained her cup and cheered.

* * * *

It all began on a rainy summer afternoon. Charlene remembered that she'd had to knock loudly on her neighbor's front door. Finally the door opened a crack, revealing a large woman wearing jeans and a baggy shirt. Her face was lined and her hair had been dark once, but was now streaked with gray. Her solid build and steady, dark eyes reminded Charlene of the women she had known in her own family. They were a strong, unbending lot that thrived here between the river and the mountain.

"So, you're the new neighbor. I'm Juanita Sweet. Come in." The woman's low, husky voice carried a hint of command. Her dark eyes weighed up Charlene carefully.

"If it wouldn't be too much trouble, I'd like to use your phone. My cell battery is dead." Charlene was exhausted from the move and Juanita Sweet's scrutiny unnerved her. She was ready to give up the idea of confronting her ex-husband on the phone, even though this was her last hope.

"Sure." Juanita smiled and led the way back to a small, neat kitchen. "You're from around here, ain't you honey?"

"Yes, but I've been away for a few years. I'm Jackson and Iva Lu Browns' daughter.

Juanita nodded. "I know your family—almost married one of your uncles. Too bad about your folks; I was at the funeral." She reached over and patted Charlene's arm. "You done the right thing to bring your kids home where you belong. Raising them by yourself in the city wouldn't have been easy." She gestured to a mobile phone. "You make that call and I'll brew us up a fresh pot of coffee."

While Charlene called Bert's number down in Richmond, she watched Juanita moving purposefully around the kitchen. The large woman's presence was comforting. When Bert answered, his reaction to her plea was predictable. By the time she hung up on him, she was furious.

Juanita guided her to a chair and set a cup of coffee in front of her. "Bastard," she hissed. "You done good to leave him." They sat in silence for a while.

"I've got leads on a couple of jobs," Charlene finally said. "But I owe the landlord now and I'm flat broke."

"Don't worry about no rent. The landlord's my uncle. He owns this place too." Juanita smiled reassuringly. "He'll wait. But that ex-husband of yours needs some grief."

* * * *

"C'mon over," Juanita urged over the phone a few days later. "Bring the kids, Charlene. I'm just gonna grill up some ribs for the gang."

Charlene heard the thump of country music blasting from the neighboring yard and walked over. Juanita's friend, Dixie, was no surprise—another country girl from Romney, West Virginia. Dixie was sprawled out on one of Juanita's rickety lounge chairs. Her long, tanned legs were propped up on the corner of the picnic table. "So, Charlene," she asked, "how does it feel to be back home?"

"Good, but everything's changed here. Do you feel that way when you go back to Romney?"

"Romney? Left that place after high school and don't go back at all unless I haveta. Followed a man down here, but I got tired of listening to him so I just walked out." Dixie paused, staring off at the mountain ridges. "Since then I've heard alotta promises from alotta different men."

The screen door banged and Juanita, laden down with a jug of wine and bags of chips, headed toward them. "Hey Charlene, glad you could make it. Where's the kids?" she yelled, trying to make herself heard over the thumping country music.

"Left them with Aunt Flo. I needed to get out."

Juanita nodded "Yeah, well you need a night out after what you just been through with that bastard of a ex-husband. Don't worry, a pretty girl like you won't have no trouble finding a man. Here, have a little wine."

Juanita was pouring the second round of Merlot when a newcomer joined the group. Charlene had watched her park the black Ford Bronco in the driveway and head toward them. Her long, tie-dyed skirt swayed and her bracelets jangled with each sandaled step.

"This here is Sylvia." Juanita waved her hand in introduction. "She's come up here to Morgan County a couple of years back to make pots and promote vegetarianism. Poor thing can't cook worth a shit, so I give her a hot meal from time to time."

"Hi, hope you like it here." Sylvia's smile was open and friendly. She was a tall, slender woman with long auburn hair done in one smooth braid. But behind her smile, Charlene picked up on the tense way Sylvia held her body.

"Nice to meet you. I grew up around here, so there won't be any big surprises. Are you from D.C. or Baltimore?" Charlene asked.

Sylvia grinned wryly. "I haven't managed to blend in yet, have I? I'm from the D.C. area. Are you looking around for a job? I've gotten to know some of the shopkeepers in town, so maybe I could help."

"I'll take you up on that offer," Charlene said. "I've left applications at a couple of places, but I've been expecting my Ex to send money for the boys."

"Ha! Don't hold your breath," Dixie chimed in. "Have you tried over at the factory yet? I met Juanita when I was looking for work at the sewing factory."

"Looking for work!" Juanita stood up and moved toward Dixie. "First time I saw Dixie, she looked like a down and out hooker. Skirt up to here—midriff top up to there." Juanita made exaggerated hand motions and minced along on imaginary high heels. "I never used no sewing machine before, but what the hell, just hand that sucker here," she said in a breathy voice.

Dixie jumped up on the picnic table and pantomimed Juanita, swinging her hips and striking poses. "Just lead me to that machine. I can do any job in this here factory." She looked around at her cheering audience, thrust her hips forward and purred, "I can do you too, Bubba." She bowed and climbed down amid laughter and clapping. "The old fart still didn't give me no job."

"I was there and she ain't exaggerating all that much," Juanita said.

"I really didn't want none of that routine factory shit, so Juanita put me on to cleaning houses. There's enough money in it for me and I set my own hours. It ain't so bad."

Juanita passed a large bowl of chips. "And you ain't even got around to your dazzling social life yet."

"Dazzling, shit! Men around here are about as piss poor as they were back in Romney. Mind, I ain't saying I don't like men."

"Well, I hate every one of them," Sylvia said. "A month ago Lloyd was crazy about me and was going to represent me in the divorce at no charge." Sylvia jumped to her feet and moved quickly around the table scooping up chips and salsa.

"That don't sound like the Lloyd I know." Juanita poured her another glass of wine.

Sylvia took the glass and leaned against the table. "Well, he's handled the divorce all right, but he's dumped me. He's living with a red-headed bimbo and I'm out in the cold." She sipped her wine, then continued. "Now he's had the nerve to send a bill. That jerk claims I owe him three thousand dollars. I can't stand his duplicity."

"Duplicity? What the hell does that mean, Sylvia?" Dixie asked.

"She's talking about double-dealing, but that ain't nothing, honey," Juanita said. She gestured toward a pile of white sand in the corner of the yard. "You talk about bastards. Well, that pile of sand is the last thing my ol' man ever gave me—and he got it free when he worked at the sand mine," she said in a low voice. "He was supposed to build me a cement patio, but about that time he cut out with my best friend, Molly."

Juanita got up and walked over to the pile of sand. Hands on hips, she kicked at it. "Look at us, girls, we're sitting in the dirt."

"We ain't only sitting in the dirt, we're sitting in the shit." Dixie stood up and walked over to the sand pile.

Kneeling down, Juanita ran the grains through her fingers. "You know, it's just about time we done something about it."

"Like what?" Sylvia asked. "God knows I've thought about retribution."

Dixie grinned. "I like the idea of retribution. The preacher always harped on retribution. All them Old Testament boys paid the price to the Lord." Gently, she sifted the sand through her fingers into her empty cup. The two women linked arms and walked back to the picnic table.

"Retribution," Juanita rolled the word off her tongue. "It has a nice ring to it."

"Yeah," Charlene chimed in. "I like the idea of getting even. I want my ex-husband to get his. He hasn't paid child support in months."

"Yeah," Dixie said, "take your ol' man, Juanita. He definitely needs some straightening out, but let's start with that bitch, Molly. She was supposed to be a friend."

"You're damned right about Molly." Juanita's eyes narrowed into slits. "She did my hair every week. I always tipped her, too. Then she turned around and did my man."

"You can bet he didn't give her no tip," Dixie chortled.

Juanita's expression turned serious. "We can't forget my son-in-law, Joe. Jan called earlier and said that bastard wouldn't let her come over here tonight—threatened her."

Dixie snorted. "Joe thinks beating on women is a contact sport. Sonnuvabitch was probably drunk again. I'd kill him."

"Why does she put up with him?" Charlene asked. "He ought to be in jail."

"The last time he beat her, she couldn't get outta bed for two days. Now she's afraid for the little boy." Juanita's voice became a whisper. "If I ever get the chance, I will kill Joe."

"Yes," Sylvia said suddenly. "We need to make a plan. It's time for retribution!"

"Right," yelled Charlene. "It's time!"

Dixie nodded. "This is about evening up the score."

Juanita didn't say a word, she only smiled, then she dumped pretzels out of a large plastic jar and replaced them with the sand from her cup. "Retribution," she shouted. "O.K. girls, everybody get some sand and add it to the jar." She watched as each woman gathered a little sand from the pile and brought it back to the table.

"Say after me." Juanita commanded. "We're getting even, you bastards!"

In turns, the women poured their sand into the jar and chanted, "We're getting even, you bastards."

"Now all together," Juanita called as she swirled the sand in the bottom of the jar.

Four voices rose in unison. "We're getting even, you bastards!" Then the women cheered and danced wildly to the country music.

A layer of white sand covered the bottom of the jar. And that's how it all began.

* * * *

A few days later, Juanita was fixing dinner when the sheriff showed up at her door. "Well, if it ain't Jim Minns. C'mon in. How are you doing?"

"Good. And you, Juanita?" A big man in his forties, Minns settled his bulk in one of the small kitchen chairs.

"Working too damn hard, but I'm O.K."

The sheriff cast an appraising eye over her. "Well, you look good."

"Thanks. How about some coffee, Jim?"

The sheriff looked at her steadily. "This ain't exactly a social call, Juanita."

Juanita kept her gaze steady as the silence lengthened.

"This here's the thing," Jim Minns said uneasily. "There's been some trouble over at Molly Finch's place. You know anything about it?"

"About what? I ain't had nothing to do with that bitch for months."

Jim Minns looked at her appraisingly again. "It seems that somebody had a bunch of rats delivered to her door. Cost her a pretty penny and she's vexed."

"She's vexed, is she?" Juanita realized that her testy tone could give her away.

"She thinks you might know something about it."

"Look, Jim, if I'd been planning to even the score with Molly, she wouldn't have a hair left on her head. You know that."

A broad grin spread over the sheriff's face. "I tried to tell her this ain't your style. But all the same, stay out of her way."

* * * *

A week after the roaring success with the rats, the group was gathered around the picnic table at Juanita's place. Dixie waved a bottle of champagne. "We ain't drinking jug wine tonight, girls. We deserve champagne. So, how does it feel, Juanita?"

"It feels damn good, but we may have a problem. The sheriff was sniffing around a few days ago. Seems Molly's been whining to him."

"Does he suspect anything?" Sylvia asked.

Juanita shook her head. "No, he figures I'd have snatched her bald-headed."

"That's what you should have done," Dixie said. "Bet she's looking over her shoulder."

"Well, girls, who's next on the 'Shit List'?" Sylvia asked.

Charlene jumped up. "How about my ex-husband? He's missed sixteen months of child support."

"Sixteen months, sonnuvabitch. So far we just been having a little fun, but now we haveta get serious." Dixie had a slow way of speaking—of dragging out her words. She grinned, but it wasn't a friendly expression. "How much does this deadbeat owe?"

"Over five thousand dollars."

"That's a lot. What's he got that's worth any money?" Sylvia asked.

"He's got a big gun collection," Charlene said, "and he just bought a new Harley."

"A new Harley," Dixie mused. "What means the most to ol' Bert? How can we really piss him off? Could we sell the Harley for parts?"

"No," Juanita said quietly, "you girls got it all wrong. The question is what can we grab the easiest that we can turn over the quickest?"

"The guns," Sylvia said. "There's always a market."

Juanita grabbed the jar of sand and held out her other hand. "Here, take a hold of my hand and form a circle. Now say: 'There is nothing we can't do if we will it to be true.'" Repeating the verse, the women followed her lead and chanted as they circled to the right, then to the left.

Juanita raised the jar and swirled the sand slowly. "C'mon, girls, one more time."

Four strong voices shouted to the sky: "There is nothing we can't do if we will it to be true!"

* * * *

Skeeter waited. The moon was sliding down behind the mountain. It was late and the women hadn't come. He lit another smoke. He was far from a perfectionist in life, but he was exacting about time. His Granny McCabe had taught him young that there was a right time for everything, planting, harvesting—all of it. Damn women! He should never have agreed. Actually, Granny was in back of it all. She was Juanita's granny, too. So when Juanita asked him for help, it was hard to say no. Yawning, Skeeter reached for the pint bottle of Jim Beam he kept in the glove compartment. Damn women! Where the hell were they?

When he finally saw the headlights, Skeeter eased his tall, lean frame out of the pickup and soundlessly moved into the woods at the side of the dirt road.

As soon as the black Bronco jolted to a stop, Juanita and Dixie jumped out and shouted, "Skeeter! Where the hell are you, Skeeter."

Skeeter watched the four women drag out two heavy crates. Hunting rifles, shotguns and pistols were passed from hand to hand. They were whooping and laughing like crazy. Shit! He was tempted to take off.

"Skeeter, get your lazy ass out here." Juanita's deep voice carried into the woods.

"C'mon, Skeeter, we got a little present for you," Dixie drawled.

Well, what the hell. Skeeter sighed and stepped out onto the road. "Never know who will show up this time of night, ladies. A man can't be too careful." He grinned at them and at the crates of guns. "After all, you was late—given up on you." Skeeter hunkered down and examined the stacked weapons. Turning them over in his hands, he couldn't believe that these women had really pulled this off. But he said, "Take a lot of work filing off these serial numbers. Haveta take care. Risky peddling this stuff." He looked at the women narrowly. "You say you picked these up down in Virginia? Just how hot are they?"

"Cut the crap, Skeeter. Charlene here has two boys to feed. The money's rightfully hers anyway." Juanita advanced on him.

"See what I can do," Skeeter mumbled as he started loading the crates into his truck. He'd agreed easily for two reasons. First, he'd liked the way Charlene looked, and second, the Browning at the bottom of the crate would be worth a small fortune to a collector. He could chuck most of the other stuff in the river—much less risky that way. Filing off serial numbers—shit! He started up the pickup and headed toward town. Yeah, that Charlene was a fine-looking woman—long hair, small waist in them tight jeans, good butt. Yeah!

* * * *

Over the next week, Charlene thought from time to time about Skeeter and the guns. She hadn't heard a word from him. She'd found work as a temporary secretary in Winchester, but by the time she put gas in the car and paid the sitter, she had little money left.

Now she was picking bush beans in Juanita's garden. The day was hot and she was sweating. Straightening up at the end of the row, she came face to face with Skeeter. Startled, she stared at him. How had he snuck up on her like that? It was unnerving.

Grinning, he handed her a roll of bills. "Hope this will keep the wolf away." He watched her steadily. "Got something else for you out in the truck."

Skeeter left as silently as he had come. Charlene stared at the wad of one hundred dollar bills. She was still in the same spot when Skeeter reappeared, bringing a string of good-sized perch. She watched his long, easy strides as he approached. She smiled, trying to overcome the uneasiness he caused her.

He shot her a cocky grin. "Think we can talk Juanita into throwing these here beauties in the frying pan? I'm starving." Skeeter continued to smile at her.

Charlene, still carrying the bucket of beans, found herself following along behind him. "Wait! Skeeter, there must be over three thousand dollars here. Thank you."

"Yeah, a little over three. Pleasure doing business with you."

"This is a Godsend. I was almost broke. What do I owe you?"

"Owe me?" Skeeter turned and his grin broadened. "Nothing, really. I was glad to help out. Hard times ain't no fun. And you're the type woman who oughta be having a little fun outta life."

Skeeter neglected to mention that his cut had been more. He needed it. You couldn't impress a new woman without cash in your pocket.

Charlene's eyes followed the swaying line of fish. She found herself staring at Skeeter's narrow hips and the rippling movement of his thighs through the faded jeans. What was wrong with her? She knew the man was no damn good, no matter what effect he had on her.

In the kitchen, Dixie, Sylvia and Juanita were cold-packing beans and putting them in the canner. The countertops were lined with bottles of green beans.

"Well, if it ain't Skeeter," Juanita said. "Come in and give us a hand with the beans."

Skeeter set the fish in the sink, then pulled a bottle of Jim Beam from his jacket pocket. "Brought ya a gift, ladies."

"Mighty generous, Skeeter. Don't recall ya being all that generous in the past. What's changed?" Juanita eyed him closely.

"Can't a man have a 'giving heart'?"

"Gifts are welcome any time, honey. Can you stay while I fry up them fish?"

He winked at Charlene and sat down at the table.

* * * *

Skeeter took off right after dinner, saying he had business to attend to. The women still sat around the table finishing off the bottle of Jim Beam. They were mixing it with Coke.

"What's this 'bout tending to business? Ever since I've known the man, he ain't even had a job." Dixie swirled the drink around in her glass and shot Charlene a sidelong glance. "Skeeter ain't a bad guy, but he hits on anything soft and sweet. I useta hang around with him." She smiled knowingly.

"Shut up, Dixie." Juanita stood up, towering over the table. "Who ain't you hung around with?" Her large bulk was threatening. "And I don't know about soft, but you ain't never been sweet. They'll be no more of them type remarks."

Charlene's face reddened. "Skeeter just handed me a wad of cash for the guns. I was in a bind." She pushed away from the table and stood up. "I've gotta check on the boys," she said and hurried into the next room where they were asleep on the couch. Let Dixie tease her, she thought. The man meant nothing to her.

Charlene was just about to re-enter the kitchen when she heard Juanita's deep voice. "What's the matter with you, Dixie? That girl's got it hard enough. We gotta stick together."

"Yeah, you're right. But face it, Juanita, even though Skeeter's your cousin, he ain't no good. Never was."

"Well, I ain't defending the boy. I gotta tell Charlene that tight buns and bedroom eyes ain't all there is. But she won't listen."

Rapping at the porch door kept Charlene in the hall. She heard Juanita call out a greeting and a man's voice reply, "Evening, Ladies. I'm afraid this is another official type call."

"Sit down, Sheriff. Have a little drink. We're mixing Jim Beam and Coke."

"Some other time, ladies. I've come to see Charlene. Her aunt said I'd find her here."

Charlene fought down the panic. She couldn't run, so she'd have to brazen it out. Just like the other women had told her—Bert would suspect her, but he'd have no proof. She entered the kitchen.

"Evening, Charlene. How've you been?"

Jim Minns looked friendly enough, although Charlene was surprised that he'd gotten heavier and was balding. She remembered that he'd been a friend of her father's.

"Fine, Sheriff. You wanted to see me?" She tried to keep her voice steady.

"There's been a little trouble down at Bert's. Has he called you?"

"No, I haven't heard from him in months."

"Seems his gun collection has been stolen. He's hopping mad," Jim Minns said.

"The whole collection's gone?" Charlene began to feel sick.

Jim nodded. "So he says. Where were you last Wednesday?"

"She was here with us," Dixie's voice cut in.

"Is that right, Charlene?" the sheriff asked.

"That's right, Jim," Juanita said. "We were all together."

"Charlene?" The sheriff's voice was firm.

Looking at the strength in the women's faces, Charlene found her own. "Yes, we were all together," she said.

Minns looked relieved. "I remember Bert was a hotheaded kid who caused trouble in high school. I was surprised you stayed with him as long as you did. Now he has some crazy notion you could have been involved."

"Sheriff," Charlene said, "I weigh 120 pounds. How could I have toted off all those guns?" She smiled shyly. "Bert owes me sixteen months in back child support. Is there anything you can do to help me?"

"It's complicated now he's down in Virginia, but I'll see what I can do. Sorry to have bothered you." As Jim Minns turned to leave, he hesitated, picked up the jar of sand on the table and examined it. "One night I'll invite you pretty ladies for a drink," he said as he left.

The women sat in stunned silence. Finally Dixie said, "Whataya think? Is he on to us?"

"It's hard to tell with Jim," Juanita looked serious. "Just don't spend none of that money too quick, Charlene."

* * * *

A week later Charlene had not been arrested, so she began to relax a little. When she arrived at Juanita's, the women were sitting around the picnic table. "Come on in, Charlene," Juanita called. "Sylvia just dragged in a box of bargains from her yard sale."

"I sat out on my lawn all day and hardly sold a thing." Sylvia scattered a few tie-dyed scarfs on the table. "Here, take anything you want. I pawned my camera last week, so I've still got a few bucks."

"Money that tight?" Juanita asked.

"I'd be doing O.K. if it weren't for that puffed up little bastard, Lloyd. Now he's threatening me with a collection agency. There ought to be something I can do."

Charlene opened the bottle of wine she'd brought and handed Sylvia a cup. "There is something you can do. Lloyd needs to suffer the way you are suffering."

The women nodded in agreement. "Yeah, that's the truth," Dixie said.

"This is just an idea, but I have a friend who works at a medical lab in D.C. Her husband ran off with an eighteen-year-old stripper and she might be mad enough to help us." Charlene offered.

"Medical lab, eh?" A slow grin spread over Juanita's face. "And you say Lloyd has got hisself a new honey?"

"That redheaded bimbo, Brenda—twenty-two years old." Sylvia smiled. "The girl's not too smart, but smart enough to steer away from certain medical conditions!" She pounded the flat of her palm down on the table. "You've got it, Juanita. You're a genius. The only question is just how serious old Lloyd's condition should be—syphilis, gonorrhea, herpes 2, what?"

"What about the redhead?" Dixie cut in. "Don't she deserve no notification? God knows what she could have by now."

"Wait a minute," Juanita's deep voice warned. "This is risky. Are you sure your friend at the lab will do it?"

Charlene nodded. "She's an ace with computers, smart enough to pull this off and never even be suspected. When she hears this story, she'll do it, but we'd need to know when Lloyd had his last physical exam."

"That's easy," Sylvia said. "He boasted that Doc Burns checked him out every year on his birthday and told him he was in great shape and could keep on smoking. No problem."

"When's his birthday?" Charlene asked.

"It's some time at the end of May. When I was seeing him last year, the old fart expected a 'special present.' Ha!" Dixie grinned. "It's on public record. We'll get the date."

Sylvia still looked skeptical. "Remember, ol' Lloyd's a lawyer. He isn't just gonna roll over with this."

Juanita laughed out loud. "C'mon, Lloyd may be a lawyer, but he's still a man. There're some things he won't want the world to know." She grabbed the jar of sand from the table. "Don't worry, this is just the beginning, girls. By the time we're done with Lloyd, he'll be begging for mercy."

"Yeah," Charlene said, "he'll be begging for mercy."

"Begging for mercy," Dixie shouted.

"Begging for mercy," Sylvia shouted.

Juanita held the jar up high and nodded to the others. "He'll be begging for mercy, but we ain't got no mercy!"

* * * *

Lloyd Watson couldn't believe his eyes. Had there been a storm last night? He would certainly have remembered a storm severe enough to bring that tremendous limb down on the roof of his new Jeep Cherokee. A huge dent now creased the shiny red finish. He wondered if he'd be able to open the door on the driver's side. His neighbor had seen an old black Bronco in the neighborhood yesterday evening. Sylvia? He shuddered. He should have never gotten mixed up with that woman.

Just as the tow truck left with the Jeep, the phone rang. The high, demanding voice of his ex-wife shrilled, "Where the hell's my check, Lloyd? According to that financial report

I received on you, you can afford to pay me twice as much, you bastard!"

"Report," Lloyd gurgled. "What report?"

"How the hell should I know where it came from; but I'm telling my lawyer to file for a new alimony hearing. Unlike you, I have to pay a lawyer now, you asshole." Her breathing sounded ragged and shallow. "To think, you've been sending me this pittance all these years. They'll be hell to pay, asshole!"

Lloyd dropped the phone, put his head in his hands and wept. How could all this be happening to him? HIM?

Later that day, Lloyd got a ride to town with his neighbor, old Mrs. Nesbitt. He had to sit in the back amidst piles of old newspapers and smelly re-cycling. Missy and Mister Fussy, the two miniature poodles, took up the front seat. He didn't reach his office until almost noon.

* * * *

Sitting at his desk reading mail, Lloyd held up an envelope and studied it. Marked "Personal," the letter was from Sylvan Medical Laboratory in Washington, D.C. He opened it and started reading: 'In reference to your last physical examination, the following tests…'

"Oh, my God!" Lloyd shouted and looked down at his lap in horror. Then he reached into a desk drawer, pulled out a whiskey bottle and took a couple of gulps.

Persistent tapping on the door finally got his attention. Dixie, wearing short shorts, a halter top, and high-wedged heels, moved toward him.

"Lloyd, I see you got the same notification. Half the ladies in the county may need to checked out, eh?" She waved a letter at him.

"Why are you here?"

"I'm here as a friend. I guess your new redheaded playmate should know about this."

"Brenda?" Lloyd sighed. "She's left me. In fact, she's left town. I had wondered why."

Dixie reached into her handbag and took out a small jar. "You ain't asked, but even though you and me were friendly in the past, I feel just fine. I've already used Granny's cure."

"There's a cure that doesn't involve doctors and clinics?"

"I got it right here." Dixie handed him the jar. "It's a mixture of tar and ginseng—works like a charm."

"How exactly does it work?"

"You don't drink it, honey. It's an ointment." Dixie smiled encouragingly. "Of course, you'll get a little rash."

"Oh, my God!" Again, Lloyd's eyes slid toward his lap.

"And sometimes you get a little itch, but it's a small price to pay," Dixie said as she turned to leave.

Lloyd sat with his head in his hands. He had been a happy man until now. His frank, open smile had convinced judge and jury alike of his absolute honesty and the innocence of his clients. This run of rotten luck could be bad for business. What if people on the street started looking at him funny? What if the whole damn town found out? What about Mother?

* * * *

The girls were blanching and skinning a bushel of tomatoes and Juanita was cold-packing them. "I saw ol' Lloyd in town the other day. He looked terrible," Juanita said. "No more 'Mister handsome big shot'."

"Well, he still looks too good. He's got himself a new girlfriend and I still have to pay his outrageous bill," Sylvia said.

"A new woman—already? Must be from outta town." Dixie placed more full bottles in the canner.

"Yeah, she's not local," Juanita said. "I seen him with her at the Food Lion—buying artichoke hearts. She was tall, skinny and snooty."

"She's a lawyer from D.C. named Melissa Thomas." Watching the faces turned toward her, Sylvia colored. "Well, I still hear things. He's known her for a couple of weeks.

About this time he'll invite her out for a day on his new speed boat—cruising the river with an ice chest full of French wine and imported cheese."

"Cruising," Dixie said slowly. "What if ol' Lloyd had a few problems on the water? What would that snazzy D.C. lawyer think of him then, huh?"

"She'd probably think he's as much of an ass as I think he is," Sylvia said. "All we have to do is wait until her car shows up at his place on a Friday night. The cruise will be on for the next day and I know his favorite picnic spot."

* * * *

"If my boat goes, I go," Skeeter said. "That's all there is to it."

"You mean you don't trust us none," Dixie taunted.

"Damn right! You're the craziest bunch of females I ever had to deal with." He started walking toward his truck.

"Oh, c'mon, Skeeter." Juanita started after him. "You done known me all your life."

"Yeah, well you've changed." Hands on his hips, he stood looking at them.

"You're right," Charlene said. "How many can fit in the boat?" She was determined to be one of the boat crew with Skeeter.

"No more 'n three, and that there is pushing it. What the hell are you women up to this time?"

"It's for Sylvia. She's got a little problem," Dixie drawled.

"Little problem." He walked back over to them. "That there woman is crazier than the rest of ya put together. Never have liked her none."

"Listen, Skeeter," Charlene said, "Sylvia helped me when I had problems. I just can't dump her now."

"No? Well I sure as hell can. Her and her crazy schemes are gonna land the whole lot a you in Regional Jail. Be nobody to look after them poor little boys." Skeeter looked hard at Charlene.

She was surprised at his concern. "This isn't gonna be risky. We're just gonna set Lloyd Watson's new boat adrift. Then he'll look like a fool in front of his new lady friend."

"Yeah, the worst that can happen is that ol' Lloyd'll haveta hoof it back to the main road through the briars and poison ivy," Dixie said. "Serves the sonnuvabitch right!"

"Lloyd Watson!" Skeeter snorted. "Why didn't ya say so? Poison ivy 'n snake bite is too good for that smartass. He took my Cousin Jason's case. Now he's in prison for life. Some lawyer!"

* * * *

Lloyd Watson felt better than he had in weeks. After the business with the bogus lab report, Mother had finally simmered down. He'd explained that mistakes like that happened in this electronic age. If the wrong birth date or initials were fed into a computer, errors would result. Too bad she'd felt she had to quit the Garden Club.

Lloyd sat leaning against a tree, watching the clear waters of the Cacapon River flow by. He'd been through a rough patch and he sure as hell had a right to a little relaxation. His flashy new boat, tied to sapling on the riverbank, was bobbing gently in the shallows.

Things had gone well since he'd met Melissa. Lloyd watched her now as she set out the delicacies packed in the picnic basket. She was a thin, knife blade of a woman, all jutting elbows and sharp edges. Her features were finely chiseled, with a straight, pointed nose and narrow, dark eyes. Not usually his type, but he liked her confidence and her haughtiness. He was due for a change. Melissa might not be hot, but she knew the right people. Her tasteful, tailored sports clothes, short stylish hair and pearl earrings were just the opposite of the wild, flamboyant outfits and bangle jewelry that bitchy-crazy Sylvia had worn. He shuddered just to think of the woman. As a matter of fact, he realized, his bad luck had started with her.

* * * *

The current ran rapidly in this part of the river, but Skeeter swung his boat expertly into the shore. Charlene and Dixie, carrying a hunting knife, jumped out and waded toward the riverbank. They moved quietly toward Lloyd's sleek boat, which was tied up near a patch of tall grass. Dixie was able to get close enough to hack through the mooring line until the craft was set free.

* * * *

Busy with his own thoughts, Lloyd had been nodding and smiling, but not listening to Melissa's conversation until she grabbed his arm. "Lloyd, the boat is floating away! It's heading downstream!"

Looking up, Lloyd gasped. "Oh, my God!" He ran to the riverbank in time to see his new boat, now caught in the current, round a bend in the river and disappear. He ran along the shore, only to watch the boat move quickly out of sight. Shocked, he turned back toward Melissa. Eyeing her trim shorts and flimsy sandals in a new light, he wondered how he'd ever get her over miles of rough, trackless wilderness to the road. He wondered how he'd make it himself. How could this have happened to him?

* * * *

Skeeter dragged the 'Road Closed' sign over to block the narrow back road that ran along the river. Never much traffic here anyway, he thought. How the hell did he keep getting himself mixed up with these crazy women? He leaned against the side of the pickup and pulled out a smoke. "Charlene don't want me to smoke, neither," he muttered to himself. Well, some things he would do, and some things he wouldn't. For a man who'd never cared for responsibility, he was sure as hell headed down a rocky road. A woman and two young 'uns—he had to be crazy.

Further down the same deserted road, Sylvia sat cross-legged under a tree. The battered black Bronco was parked nearby. Sweating, she waved her large straw hat at the swarms of bugs. It was hot as hell, but sitting in the shade had to beat tramping through the woods. She grinned.

* * * *

"Lloyd, do you have any idea where you're going?" Melissa demanded. "We've been stumbling around in this swamp for hours."

Batting away insects, Lloyd puffed and wheezed. "I've never had to do this on foot before. Just head toward the mountain; I think that's north."

Melissa marched on, trying to avoid most of the briars. "For God's sake, you're the country boy, aren't you? Do I have to drag you along?"

Lloyd's fair skin was blotched with puffy bug bites. He was limping. "My new boat, my baby," he moaned. "After all I've been through in the last few weeks, I should have expected something like this to happen to me."

"You've told me, Lloyd. You've made it sound like some sort of witch hunt. Come on!" Melissa shoved him and moved purposefully ahead. "You forget that I work as a public defender in D.C. I hear real horror stories every day." She snorted. "I don't have a fat cat backwater practice like you."

Lloyd trashed through the woods, stumbling over tangled roots and brambles. When a large snake slithered across the path in front of him, he screamed and collided with Melissa who came up from behind. "Snake!" he shrieked.

"Oh, for Chrissakes," she rasped. "It's only a black snake. Down in D.C. I have to dodge rats as big as cats in the projects where my clients live." She curled her hands into claws and raked the air in front of him.

"That's not funny," he moaned and thought her narrow, sharp features had a rodent-like quality. He was stuck in the wilderness with Rat Woman.

* * * *

When they finally reached the road, it was almost dark. Lloyd fell down in the weeds and assorted trash by the road-side. Melissa loomed over him. He couldn't see her face in the twilight, but her posture looked threatening. Damn, Lloyd thought, what was the bitch's problem. He'd gotten her to the road, hadn't he?

"Funny, no cars have gone by," he finally said. She didn't answer.

Several minutes later, Melissa pointed and started waving wildly. "There, a car is coming!" The black Bronco slowly moved down the road and stopped.

"Oh, for Chrissakes," Lloyd moaned. He thought of refusing the ride, but Melissa had already climbed in the front seat. He felt doomed. He would rather have slept on the side of the road. Finally, he heaved himself into the back seat in time to hear Melissa's strident accusations.

"…and this wuss couldn't even find the path. We'd still be wandering around out there if I hadn't dragged him here."

"Yes, I know him," Sylvia agreed calmly. "He brings trouble down on himself. He's like a huge raincloud," she murmured.

They had gone two or three miles when the Bronco bumped to a halt. It was now completely dark. There was not even a moon. Strangest of all, Lloyd thought, they hadn't passed a single car in either direction.

Sylvia fiddled with the ignition and hammered on the in-strument panel with her fist. "Out of gas," she said.

They sat in silence for a while. Lloyd spent the time digging at his mosquito bites. He found it difficult to string thoughts together anymore.

"Well," Melissa said tersely, "what are you waiting for, Lloyd. We need gas."

Lloyd limped down the road. Actually, he was glad to be out of the car and away from both women. There was some quality about them that made him extremely uneasy. His asthma had started up again.

* * * *

"Mary Liz over at the Food Lion says she's never seen women buying so much champagne," Sylvia chortled as she filled up the glasses then passed them out to the gang assembled at Juanita's picnic table.

"Well, God knows we deserve it," Dixie said. "Show us that there legal paper again, Sylvia."

Sylvia waved a piece of notebook paper over her head and danced around the table. "Melissa turned out to be an amazing woman. This is all her handiwork." She shook the paper. "When she heard my story, she said there were a few legal agreements Lloyd and I should have reached before he sent me that outrageous bill. So when the bastard finally got back with the gas, we were ready for him."

Charlene carefully put the paper in her purse. "I thought Melissa was just another snobby bitch, but she's one of us. Poor old Lloyd actually looked glad to sign and get away from both of us. Now he's released me from all debt."

"All right, Sylvia, you stuck it to that puffed up little jerk. Lloyd ain't gonna look so prissy-ass smart no more," Juanita said.

"It feels good, don't it?" Dixie raised her glass. "To Sylvia," she said.

"It feels great!" Sylvia yelled to make herself heard over the cheering. "Who's next, girls? We're just beginning to rock and roll."

"I been hearing a lot about Chet Monroe lately. None of it good." Dixie's tone was serious. "He's turned into a real badass."

"Dealing drugs?" Charlene asked.

"You bet. He's pedaling that shit to middle school kids now."

"And that ain't all, is it, Dixie?" Juanita said.

"That ain't the half of it. Chet and I go way back. He's the man I followed down here from Romney. Only I ain't never told you girls the truth." She hesitated. "He wasn't so bad back then—just drank a little too much booze and cut deals on hot car parts."

"C'mon, Dixie, you might as well finish the story," Juanita coaxed.

"The truth is Chet dumped me, not the other way 'round. Left me with a load of bills and not as much as a 'so long.' The law ransacked the trailer, accused me of heisting cars. I'd like to see him go away for a long time."

"In that case," Charlene said. "We need to set him up."

"Now you're talking." Juanita nodded. "Ain't your cousin the bartender down at the County Line Bar?"

"He's been there a while," Charlene agreed.

Juanita looked serious. "We need to know when Chet usually hits the bar, how long he stays and what he drinks."

"I'll tell ya right now, he's a bar fly and an easy drunk," Dixie drawled. "This is gonna be a cinch."

"Here, take a holda my hand, girls." Juanita stretched her arm across the table and the others followed her lead. "Here's to swatting flies," she said.

"Yeah!" the women yelled and cheered for Dixie.

* * * *

A jukebox blared county music at the County Line Bar. The women, dressed to kill in an abundance of flashy spandex and gaudy jewelry, were drinking red wine at a table near the door. A round had already been sent over by one of the men at the bar. Dixie nudged Juanita as Chet Monroe walked through the swinging doors. When he noticed the women, he headed for their table.

"Well, if this ain't a surprise. You girls are looking good. Especially you, Dixie." He smiled and put his hand on her shoulder.

"Looking good yourself, Chet. Let me introduce my friends."

"Only got a minute, girls. Got an appointment, but what the hell." Chet pulled up a chair next to Dixie and ordered a drink.

After the first round, Chet loosened up a little and flashed the women his winning smile. "I'm on top of the world." His voice was smooth. "I'm sitting with the best looking women here."

"Saw that fancy new vehicle you're driving, Chet. Business must be booming," Juanita said.

"Yeah, got two more roofing jobs lined up today."

"Roofing jobs," Dixie snorted. "You're a piece a work, Chet."

"What you talking 'bout. I'm a hard-working man."

"There's only one thing you ever worked hard at." Dixie winked at him.

"There's a couple of things that would fit in that category, and one makes me think of you," he replied. "C'mon, let's dance."

"Actually, those two look pretty good together. He's a good-looking guy." Charlene observed as she watched the dancers. "Too bad he's such a shit."

"He ain't so pretty if you know him," Juanita said. She glanced at her watch and made a call on her cell phone. "Excuse me a minute, girls."

Grabbing her large handbag, she got up and headed across the dance floor. As she passed Chet and Dixie, she tripped and crashed into them. The two women landed on the floor.

"Oh, my God," Juanita cried. "I feel like I been hit by a freight train." She looked around for her handbag.

Chet reached down and helped Juanita up. "Sorry. Dixie here always was clumsy. You O.K.?"

Juanita nodded and struggled to her feet.

Dixie had already scrambled up and handed the bag to Juanita. "Here. Ain't this yours? You don't wanta forget this."

Chet looked Dixie up and down. "You doing O.K.?"

"Yeah, I'm tripping all over your big feet. They're about as big as your big mouth." Dixie grabbed his hand. "C'mon man, you gotta move them feet."

Returning to the table, Juanita pulled a ring of keys from her bag and handed them to Sylvia. "Things went good," Juanita said. "Chet doesn't even know he's lost these." She glanced around the empty table. "What happened to Charlene?"

Sylvia nodded at the pool table. "She found Skeeter."

* * * *

Charlene removed a pool cue from the rack and smiled at Skeeter. "How about a game, cowboy?"

He looked at her narrowly. "You girls are upta something and I don't like it. Chet Monroe ain't nobody t' mess with."

"You don't like it?" Charlene tossed her hair back. "Well, you're not involved."

"Charlene, you sound just like the resta them. And that ain't good."

"I thought you liked them?"

"Like 'em!" Skeeter said. "Juanita's related, but she's a bossy bitch. Sylvia's a smartass city girl and Dixie's a slut. Altogether, they're dangerous as hell." He turned and walked toward the bar.

Charlene was confused. Did Skeeter really worry for her safety or was he just another control freak? When she returned to the table, Dixie and Chet were already there.

"Charlene." Dixie gave her a penetrating look. "Sylvia here's drunk and about ready to puke. I gotta hold her hand, so you dance with Chet."

As Dixie helped Sylvia out the rear exit, Chet grabbed Charlene and led her out on the dance floor.

* * * *

Music from the bar carried out to the parking lot. "That's Chet's shiny new truck," Dixie said softly. "Here, take these latex gloves." The two women walked to the back of the lot.

Sylvia pulled on the gloves as she looked over the truck. "My brother used to sell high end cars. See that logo on the side? This is custom made and expensive."

Dixie used a key from the ring to open the door. "Chet's never made an honest dollar, so we're just helping out law enforcement." She climbed into the front seat and looked around. "Wouldn't it be a hoot if ol' Chet already had a bag of grass in here. He said he was on his way to a meet."

Dixie unlocked the glove compartment, reached in and pulled out a handgun. "Will ya look at this here—a concealed weapon. Gotcha!"

Sylvia gave her accomplice a large bag of grass and watched her shove it into the glove box with the handgun. Then Sylvia pulled a joint from her pocket.

"You lit up yet?" Dixie asked. "Here, I needa drag."

"This should be enough for 'probable cause'," Sylvia said, "but we need to hurry."

Dixie took a long drag, pinched out the end and placed the joint in the ashtray. Then the two women ran through the shadows to the bar's back door. "Goodby, Mister Candyman," Dixie called over her shoulder.

* * * *

Charlene and Chet were still dancing when Sylvia and Dixie got back to the table. Skeeter, his expression dark, his eyes menacing, stood at the bar watching the dancers.

"That boy is 'bout ready to explode," Juanita said and gestured at her cousin.

"Chet's got little Charlene in a bear hug. He deserves all the trouble coming his way." Dixie looked delighted.

When the song ended, Chet patted his partner's butt and was leaning in for a kiss when Skeeter lunged at him, dragging him away from Charlene.

"Get your hands off her, you sonnuvabitch," Skeeter yelled. "I'm gonna kill you." He landed a punch on Chet's nose.

"My God! Ya broke my nose. What the hell's wrong with you, man? You're crazy!" Chet, bleeding profusely, took a couple of swings at his opponent, then backed toward the door.

"Get him," several in the crowd yelled at Skeeter. "You ain't gonna let that bastard walk, are ya?"

Chet wasn't fast enough and Skeeter grabbed him again. "You wanta see a bear hug, you dumb shit? I got my own version."

The two men rolled on the floor. Chet's cries of pain now became calls for help, but not a soul stepped forward.

Chet finally wrangled himself free and had started to crawl toward the door, when the Sheriff and his deputy came into the bar.

"What the hell's going on here?" Jim Minns demanded.

"Monroe started it," one of the on-lookers yelled.

The Sheriff looked down at Chet, who was bloody and moaning. Then he sized up Skeeter, who stood belligerently with Juanita and her friends.

Chet heaved himself to his feet and tried to push through the door. "Thanks, Sheriff. You came just in time. These people are all crazy, so I'm getting outta here."

"You're right, Chet. You're coming with us. I got a phone tip concerning you and we needta search your vehicle, son."

"What the hell ya talking 'bout? I'm clean. Ain't nothing in my truck. I swear."

While the deputy cuffed Chet, the bartender scooped a ring of keys off the floor and handed them to Sheriff Minns. "These your keys, Monroe?" The Sheriff asked.

Struggling in the deputy's grip, Chet turned and spotted Dixie, who grinned and blew him a kiss. As the door slammed, the barkeep brought a bottle of champagne to the women's table.

* * * *

Small American flags hung from Juanita's porch posts and red, white and blue banners were draped the length of the porch. Twilight had set in, and the deep purple mountain ridges were starkly outlined against the darkening sky.

Dixie and Sylvia dragged small tree branches and kindling toward a large fire pit. "This here is a Chet Monroe fire," Dixie said as she threw wood onto the flames. "That asshole is gonna get a hot reception down at Regional Jail. I let my cousin Jake know to expect him soon." Dixie threw a large log on the fire and the two girls headed over to the picnic table. "Jake'll pass the word to the other cons that the 'Candy Man' is on his way."

"I been waiting on you two," Juanita said as she turned on the radio and country music blasted into the yard. "Let's get this party started. It's the fourth of July for God's sake." She handed the girls glasses of iced champagne.

"Where's Charlene at?" Dixie asked.

Juanita nodded toward the porch where Skeeter and Charlene leaned close together and seemed to be whispering. Charlene flipped her hair back and giggled.

"Guess Charlene ain't listening to your lectures 'bout tight buns and bedroom eyes," Dixie said.

"You surprised?"

"Hell no," Dixie said, "but that girl needs a wakeup call. I've got a plan, so Sylvia, could you take her boyfriend over a drink?" Sylvia nodded and headed to the porch.

"Thought I'd serve our guest a little bubbly." Sylvia handed a glass to Skeeter. Grinning, he took the glass and topped it off from his pint of Jim Beam.

Suddenly Dixie appeared at his side. She moved closer and spoke softly, "Remember how we spent last fourth of July? Jus' the two of us."

Skeeter grinned. "That place on the river? Oh, yeah."

"C'mon, let's dance, for old time's sake." Dixie grabbed his hand and dragged him out into the yard. He barely had time to set his drink on the porch railing. Dixie draped her arms around his neck and moved with the throbbing guitar beat, plastering her body against his. "Oh, yeah. That's the way, baby," she purred.

Charlene couldn't take her eyes off the dancers. She was surprised at their grace and the fluidness of their paired bodies. She watched as Dixie parted her lips and ran her tongue around the outline. Then she dragged her fingernails slowly down Skeeter's backbone. "My God, Dixie," she yelled. "You're shaking everything at once—just like a bitch in heat." But no one heard her.

Belting out the words to the song, Juanita and Sylvia started a wild two-step around the fire. Their performance managed to push Skeeter and Dixie even closer together. There was no moon, but the dancer's bodies threw sensual shadows from the firelight.

Charlene's face flushed hot, and suddenly she wanted Dixie's hands off him! Stomping over to the couple, she grabbed Skeeter's arm. Dixie hung on to his other arm.

"C'mon girls, no need to get greedy," Skeeter said, still smiling.

"Get your hands off him, bitch!" Charlene yelled.

"I had him first!" Dixie clung to her partner's arm.

Realizing that the fun was over, Skeeter's tone became coaxing. "C'mon Charlene, it was just a little dancing."

"Like the good ol' days, eh babe?" Dixie braced her feet and hung on.

"Ladies, calm down." A note of desperation crept into Skeeter's voice. "Charlene, honey, hey! Let go, both of ya."

Juanita was just about to intervene, when she heard the phone ringing insistently in the kitchen and headed inside.

"You whore," Charlene shrieked. "Get off him."

"Oh, shut up. Look who's talking 'bout whores." Dixie started to lose her grip and Skeeter finally shook himself free.

"That's it. Now, the both of ya, calm down," he shouted, but turned at the sound of Juanita's screams.

* * * *

The women gathered around the kitchen table where Juanita sat sobbing. Skeeter stood behind her chair. Finally, she looked up at them. "The emergency room doctor said Jan was holding her own, but Joe really worked her over this time," she said in a choked voice. "Thank God she took the boy with her. I gotta get there."

Skeeter touched her shoulder. "C'mon, babe. I'll run you in to the hospital when you're ready. Stay with you."

"Juanita," Charlene called as they were leaving, "send your grandson back with Skeeter. We'll look after him."

The women stood at the door quietly and watched the car head down the driveway, then straggled back to the kitchen table. "Has anyone ever met Jan and the little boy?" Charlene asked.

"I ain't seen them for a while. He don't let them come here," Dixie said. "There's been bad blood between Juanita and Joe for years."

"Why haven't some of the men in the family tried to straighten him out?" Sylvia looked puzzled.

"Oh, they have. Juanita's ol' man and Skeeter worked Joe over a couple a times. Made threats. Then he started boozing again and took it out worse on his wife and kid." The Champagne had gone flat, but Dixie divided it among them. "Let's drink to that sunnuvabitch. Joe's too dumb to know it, but the Devil's breathing down his neck."

* * * *

The next morning the four women sat silently in Juanita's kitchen. No one had slept. Juanita, her eyes red and swollen, finally spoke, "Last night, my grandson cried in his sleep. He saw it all. What kinda man does this?"

"The bad kind," Dixie said flatly. "We got two days before Jan will get outta the hospital. The games are over, girls. This one's for keeps."

"This is the final retribution," Charlene said.

"You know what my vote is, but I wouldn't expect none of you to help." Juanita's tone was firm. "It's for me to do."

"We're in this together. I say let's do it!" Sylvia said.

Dixie grinned. "I still got that old handgun."

None of them heard Skeeter climb the back steps. He stood listening at the screen door. "Damn, crazy women," he muttered. He studied the faces of the four women. Juanita's dark eyes were glowing hot. Sylvia's green eyes glittered coldly. Dixie's eyes were narrowed into slits. Charlene looked down at the table. He understood. They really meant to do it. Men would talk a lot, then usually have the damn good sense to leave it at that. But these women would cook up some wild scheme and they would go through with it! God help them all. He looked again at Charlene.

Entering the kitchen, Skeeter knew he was the intruder. They didn't want him there. Well, that was too damn bad. Jan and the little boy were his kin, too. He'd vowed the son-nuvabitch would pay and had his own plans.

"Ladies, he said, "if you want my opinion, what y'all have in mind is too shit good for Joe. He should be got rid of—yeah—but don't ya want him to suffer none? Don't ya want to nail him up? The man is one mean asshole and needs some grief.

Finally, Juanita looked at Skeeter. "What you got in mind?"

Skeeter breathed easier when he saw the flicker of interest in the upturned faces. "I got some friends in Baltimore," he said. "They owe me big. So, I'll head down there and set things up."

Later, after they'd worked out the details, Skeeter had to stand firm on one crucial point. "Juanita, you got to stay behind, got to be seen by a lot of people here."

Grudgingly, she agreed. She would take her grandson and Charlene's boys to the Fireman's Carnival that night.

"I gotta leave," Skeeter said and grabbed Charlene's hand. "C'mon, walk me out." At the truck, he bent down and kissed her. "I sure as hell wish you'd stay home with Juanita and the kids," he said. "This could go wrong."

"They'll need three people, Skeeter. You know that."

"Yeah, well just be careful." He held her lightly at the waist. "When this is over, we're gonna celebrate alone, just the two of us." His breath was warm on her cheek.

Charlene found the women standing by the picnic table. "C'mon," Juanita called. "There's something we gotta do. Here, girls, take a hold of my hand and make a ring." She held the big jar up, swirled the sand and placed it in the center of the ring.

"Joe, this is payback time," Juanita shouted. "We're paying you back, you bastard!"

The women circled to the right, then to the left, shouting, "We're paying you back, you bastard! We're paying you back, you bastard! You're on your way to hell!"

* * * *

The TV picture was rolling and out of focus, so Joe got up and banged on the top of the set. "Shit!" He bellowed as he lowered himself into his shabby recliner, "Can't even watch the game without some damn problem!"

He reached for his drink, but the glass was empty. He was ready to tell Jan to bring him another whiskey when he remembered that the bitch was gone. She'd grabbed the boy and taken off last night. Hell, he hadn't messed her up that bad. She'd been able to drive away, hadn't she? And in the car he'd bought and paid for. She had it too damn good. Right now she was probably sniveling around over at her mother's—complaining about him, no doubt, to the super bitch.

Joe was lumbering into the kitchen to get another drink when he heard a knock at the door. Opening it cautiously, he was amazed to find Dixie, dressed to kill, standing on the porch. She smiled and walked into the house. It was like his birthday and Christmas rolled into one. He grinned back at her.

"Hey, Joe, you in a party mood? I brought a bottle of peach brandy."

"Peach brandy. Damn. Don't know whether you or the brandy will be sweeter."

"Well, let's find out." Dixie started dancing around the room to music blasting from the half-time show on TV. Joe tried to grab her, but she stayed just out of his reach.

"I need a drink, baby," Dixie crooned.

"Sure, right away."

Joe smiled broadly as he handed his guest a drink. "You know, I ain't never believed in luck, or shit like that, but you showing up tonight is the best damn thing that's happened to me in weeks."

"You're right, your luck has changed, Joe. Let's drink to that."

Joe held up his glass, "To Dixie, the hottest little girl in Morgan County."

Joe's cell phone rang and he pulled it from his pocket. "Hang on a minute, honey. I gotta take this." He walked into the kitchen.

Dixie took a packet of white powder from her bag and slipped it into Joe's drink. Then she moved quietly to the kitchen doorway and listened. "Hello, hello," Joe said. "Hell, no. This ain't Brownie's Pizza, you idiot."

"Damn wrong number," Joe explained as he returned to the living room. "Now, where were we?"

"We were drinking." Dixie raised her glass and took a sip. Joe swigged down half of his brandy. "We were drinking to you, Joe—to the sexiest wife-beater in the county. Ain't we a pair?"

"Lay off that 'wife-beater' shit. That bitch had it coming." Joe finished his drink and moved around the room after Dixie.

"All you damn women are the same." His speech was becoming slurred. "You showed up here and now you're playing coy." Joe lurched and the glass slipped from his grasp. He hit the floor hard and his powerful body was still.

Dixie ran to open the door. "The crate's ready," Charlene said as she and Sylvia came inside. With effort, they dragged Joe out and hauled him into the back of the black Bronco.

* * * *

Two and a half hours later, the Bronco moved slowly along dockside at Baltimore harbor. His abductors dragged Joe up the gangplank to the waiting freighter. Skeeter and two Latino crewmen materialized out of the darkness and hauled Joe below deck.

When Skeeter reappeared, he flashed a grin. "Got Joe's seaman's papers. He's done signed on for three years. At midnight, the Yucatan Queen will sail for South America."

"That trip should be enough time for an attitude adjustment," Sylvia said.

"Yeah, if he ever gets back here, he'll be bitching in Spanish," Dixie drawled.

"Wait a minute." Charlene looked worried. "What if he jumps ship at the first port and heads straight back home?"

"He won't do that." Skeeter sounded confident. "It's all set up."

"I hope to hell it's foolproof," Dixie said.

"You girls worry too much. Tomorrow when Joe wakes up in his seaman's bunk, the First Mate'll bust him. I planted a few packets on Joe and passed the First Mate a "C" note. Joe'll be too damn scared to even leave the ship."

Dixie looked concerned for the first time. "I hear there isn't much that scares Joe."

"The threat of being handed over to the Mexican Federales for smuggling drugs should do it." Skeeter grinned.

"Yeah, "Dixie agreed, "Joe ain't fool enough to wanta do time in a foreign jail."

"He ought to be spending time in a West Virginia jail," Sylvia said, "but that will never happen."

"Don't worry, girls. Joe's on his way to hell."

* * * *

The drive back to Morgan County seemed to take forever. The women followed Skeeter's truck. They were triumphant, but tired, and there was little conversation. When they crossed the Potomac River Bridge into West Virginia, they were alarmed to see a road block ahead. A deputy pulled over Skeeter's truck, but waved the Bronco on to a checkpoint.

"Evening, Ladies," the State Trooper smiled appreciatively at the three women. "Y'all out late."

"Yes, sir. We had car trouble, but we're on our way home."

"Y'all better be careful now," he drawled. "We done had two convicts escape from Regional Jail this evening. May be around here." He smiled again, trying to catch Dixie's eye. "You ladies may need some protection. Ain't safe for sweet, young things like you all alone. Be sure to let me know if you have any problems." He waved them on.

Watching the deputy, Skeeter caught the glint of suspicion in his eyes. Dumbass cop thinks I might have something to do with them escapees, Skeeter thought. But that state boy is sure them women are sweet as pie.

"Where you been tonight and where you headed to?" the deputy asked.

"It ain't none of your business, but I been visiting my grandma McCabe. I gotta warn ya, she don't hear too good and she sure don't like strangers."

The officer frowned and made notes.

"Look, deputy, if ya ain't got no more questions, I'm in a hurry," Skeeter said.

As he followed the Bronco down the road toward Peach Tree Hollow, Skeeter muttered, "Hope them poor jailbirds don't stumble into Juanita's holler. Them women'll hang 'em outta dry and feed 'em to the hound dogs for supper."

Grinning, he wondered why he wasn't smart enough to take his own advice. He knew for sure he'd end up worse off than ol' Lloyd, or Bert, or even Joe if he messed up with Charlene. Them wicked women would see to it!

* * * *

It was late by the time the black Bronco reached Juanita's. She had a roaring blaze going in the fire pit and was waiting for them. "Did it go smooth?" she asked.

"Like we planned." Dixie nodded. "You called his house at just the right time."

"Listen!" Charlene raised a warning hand. "It's the news on WCST."

A police report just in from southern Morgan County: Joe McCaffrey is reported missing. His mother visited the home when he could not be reached by phone. McCaffrey's pickup truck was found in the driveway. Mrs. McCaffrey describes her son as a loving husband and father who would not willingly leave his home. McCaffrey, 32, is a white male weighing 240 pounds, 6 feet, 1 inch tall. He was awaiting trial on a domestic dispute charge. Anyone with information regarding this case is asked to call the sheriff's Office. And now we'll check the weather…

"That's the first and last time that no-good bastard will ever be famous," Dixie said.

"Yeah." Juanita smiled. "You say he was sleeping like a baby?"

Charlene nodded. "The last time we saw him, he was dead to the world."

"Too bad it ain't permanent." Juanita's expression was grim. "My girl will come home from the hospital tomorrow."

"Does she know?" Charlene asked.

"Jan knows. It was the first time she smiled," Juanita said.

"We done the right thing." Dixie pounded her fist down on the picnic table.

"It was the only thing to do," Charlene agreed. "She'd be dead if we'd waited on the law."

"Domestic violence!" Dixie laughed. "Those worthless shits file it under fiction and forget it."

Charlene looked at Juanita. "The news report doesn't worry you?"

"Hell, no." The big woman raised a dismissive hand. "Joe got a better deal than he ever deserved."

"Well, I say this calls for a celebration!" Sylvia popped the cork on a bottle of champagne.

"Wait!" Juanita said. "Where's Skeeter? He oughta be part of this. We couldn't have done it without him."

"I never thought I'd say this, but Skeeter ain't so bad." Dixie poured out the champagne.

"Men in general ain't so bad, once you weed out the bastards," Juanita said.

Dixie jumped up on the picnic table and held up the champagne bottle. "That's what we done, girls. We weeded out the bastards!" She waved the bottle.

Juanita stood up. "Girls, put your right hand on the jar and raise your cup," she shouted, "We weeded out the bastards!"

The women called back in unison, "We weeded out the bastards!"

Amid the cheering and whooping, a new voice shouted, "Wait. I want in." Molly Finch, sporting a black eye, joined them.

Juanita looked shocked. "My God, Molly! What the hell you doing here?"

"You got a damn nerve." Dixie stepped forward.

"Let's hear her out," Juanita said calmly.

Molly ran over and threw her arms around Juanita. "I've come to apologize. I was dead wrong. You were the best friend I ever had."

"What happened to your eye?" Juanita asked.

Molly put her hand up to the red, puffy area around her eye. "Well, a couple of hours ago I got socked in the face by a scrawny little rooster. Not your man, Juanita. He walked out after the rats was dumped."

"Sounds like him," Juanita said.

"This here's the thing." Molly looked nervous. "I know I ain't got no right to ask, but y'all got something powerful going on. You take care of business and I want in."

"Well, you're crazy," Dixie snorted.

"Hold on, It took some guts to come here tonight," Juanita said. "She's got my vote."

"Mine, too," Charlene weighed in.

"Yeah, why not?" Sylvia said.

"Yeah, I guess." Dixie didn't look convinced.

Molly started to cry. "I swear you won't regret it."

"Here." Juanita handed her a cup. "Stop bawling and fill the cup with sand from that pile. Don't spill a drop!"

The others walked behind Molly and filled their cups with sand.

"Now," Juanita commanded. "Follow us. Repeat what we say and mean it."

Molly watched as the women poured sand into the large jar, then she followed suit. Juanita lifted up the jar as the others held hands and circled her.

"We're getting even, you bastards!" the women yelled as they moved to the right, then to the left.

"C'mon, girls." Dixie waved the champagne bottle. "We got more bubbly."

* * * *

When Charlene saw Skeeter standing on the porch, she went over and stood beside him. "My God," he said. "Them women have turned into a scary bunch."

"Then why did you help us?" she asked.

"Why? Because of family, because Joe deserved it, and because of you, Charlene. I couldn't see you risk jail time."

"You're late." Charlene took his hand. "I've been worried about you, too."

"Had a little run-in with the sheriff on the way home. Has he been here yet?"

"No, but we heard the radio news report. Is there trouble?"

Charlene and Skeeter turned and watched as the sheriff walked around the side of the house and headed toward the picnic table.

"Evening, ladies. Drinking champagne, I see." He looked around at the women.

"Evening, Jim. Care to join us?" Juanita asked.

"Why not." He sat down, taking up one end of the bench. I'm surprised to see you here, Molly. What happened to you?"

"Oh, I had a misunderstanding with a little jerk, Sheriff, but it'll be taken care of now." She picked up the jar, now half full of sand, and tilted it back and forth. The fine white sand flowed like water. "Juanita and I are tight again. I figure I been a damn fool complaining 'bout my best friend in the world."

The sheriff also watched the swirling sand. "Juanita, I'm sorry to hear about your girl. You know how I feel about that kinda thing." He looked her in the eye. "Guess you heard that Joe disappeared?"

"We heard a news report on the radio."

"I see," Jim Minns said. "Mind if I ask where you ladies were tonight?"

"I was at the Firemen's Carnival with my grandson and Charlene's boys." Juanita said.

"And where were the rest of you ladies?"

"Charlene, Sylvia and I visited my granny up in Romney." Dixie smiled winningly.

"I'm sure if I ask Granny, she'll vouch for you." Jim Minns picked up the jar of sand and turned in thoughtfully in his hands. "Strange. This is the third time I've visited you ladies recently."

"We love to see you, Sheriff," Dixie said.

"If I was a gambling man, I'd say those are good odds that something's going on here." Jim Minns set the jar down and looked hard at the women. "Joe may have been a sonnuvabitch, but now he's missing, and that's serious."

Juanita stared back at the sheriff. "I can't say I'm sorry he's gone. Maybe he just took off rather than face his day in court."

"Juanita, I know you hated him, and I know you had reason. But, I'll have to keep investigating. Remember, I keep an open door if you need to talk." The sheriff got up, tapped the sand container one more time and walked toward the driveway. "Goodnight, ladies. I know I don't have to tell y' all to be good."

After the sheriff left, Charlene and Skeeter came down to the picnic table. Charlene looked nervous, but Skeeter grinned. "That man don't have a clue. You women worry too much. Ain't gonna be that many people even miss Joe McCaffrey."

"I hope you're right," Juanita said. "but we couldn't have done it without you. Thanks, Skeeter."

"It was a job that needed doing." Skeeter grinned and took Charlene's hand. "I'm gonna help this girl get her kids off your couch and into their beds. 'Night, ladies."

* * * *

The women pulled up chairs around the fire. "My God, I thought the sheriff would never leave," Molly said.

"So tell us what's going on, Molly," Juanita asked.

"It has to do with a man named Carmichael."

Dixie looked concerned. "Not that badass, Nate Carmichael?"

"The same," Molly said. "He sold me bargain beauty equipment that fell apart the next day. I'd paid with a credit card that got hacked. Damn shit wouldn't answer my calls, so I tracked him down at the County Line Bar tonight." She dabbed at her puffy eye. "When I raised hell, he socked me and told me to keep my mouth shut or things would get worse."

"Maybe we should pay the man a little visit," Dixie said.

"That won't be so easy. There's only three of us." Sylvia looked doubtful.

"Three's enough to make a plan." Juanita stood up.

"Three's enough to break a man." Dixie also stood.

"Teach him the error of his ways." Sylvia joined them.

"Reckon up his sinful days," Juanita said.

"But four can make a plan a fact." Molly stepped forward.

"If we enter in a pact." Juanita picked up the heavy jar of sand.

The women held hands and circled around the fire. Juanita raised the jar high, then took a handful of sand and tossed it over the flames. "There is nothing we can't do, if we will it to be true," she cried.

One after another, the women threw handfuls of sand into the blaze. Their circle reversed direction and their chants became louder. "There is nothing we can't do, if we will it to be true!" Juanita lifted the jar high, then scattered the rest of the sand to the four winds.

The women's chants drifted over the mountain ridges like the smoke from the fire. Their message reached every hollow in the valley and intruded into Joe McCaffrey's drugged dreams at sea. "There is nothing we can't do, if we will it to be true!" It was a cry that carried power and carried hope.

EPILOGUE

A few days later, Jan got a phone call from the Florida State Police. The U.S. Coast Guard had found her husband floating off the coast on a piece of driftwood. He had pled innocence regarding the large amount of drugs he'd been carrying. Joe McCaffrey claimed that relatives in West Virginia had kidnapped him and left him in the hands of cutthroats. He had escaped at great risk and should be welcomed as a hero as he had kept drugs out of the hands of thieves and warlords.

However, it was found that West Virginia had issued a bench warrant on McCaffrey for failure to appear at a court hearing. The State of Florida agreed to return him to West

Virginia only when he had been tried on the current drug charges and fulfilled any term of punishment meted out by the Florida court. In the meantime, Joe was in jail awaiting trial. Although this news was frightening for Jan, Juanita and the other women told her not to worry. If Joe ever did return, he'd have a new attitude and be bitching in Spanish.

That Saturday night, the women invited Sheriff Minns over for a drink. The moon had risen high above the mountain ridges and the fire had burned low by the time the sheriff was drunk enough to confess his fears.

"You know I love you girls and I've been mighty worried about you." Minns glanced at the empty sand container on the picnic table.

"Jim." Juanita held up her hand. "Let me set your mind at ease. Now that Nate Carmichael has packed up and left town, we're done. You can breathe easy." The others nodded in agreement and Dixie refilled his cup.

"I wondered why Carmichael high-tailed it outta here. I gotta admit he was no loss." Jim sipped his drink. "For a while I was afraid I'd haveta throw all of you in the slammer."

Jim, let me do some explaining," Juanita said.

Jim held up his hand. "I don't want to know. If you say you're done, that's good enough for me. I'm looking forward to taking it easy for awhile, now that all the bad asses are thinking twice before they make a move."

He raised his cup. "To you—the wicked women of Peachtree Holler."

NOTHING MORE TO LOSE

Clint McCabe was riding on a freedom high most of the way up I-70. Telling that shithead foreman off was the best damn thing he'd ever done. Now each mile brought him closer to West Virginia. The radio wailed out country music and McCabe kept the beat with the flat of his hand on the dashboard. Outside Frederick, he got his first glimpse of the distant mountains. He lit a cigarette and began to relax.

He had 38 bucks and a half a tank of gas. But what the hell, he was on his way home! South of Berkeley Springs he swung left onto Route 13 and headed toward his grandfather's place. The closer he got, the more edgy he felt. How would Pap react? It would probably hinge on how much he'd had to drink. "Well shit!" McCabe shouted above the thumping beat of the guitars, "I ain't never had no damn luck, so why should it change now!"

Gospel music blasted from the radio as he pushed in the screen door and entered Pap's kitchen. The room was small and cluttered. Pap, his attention centered on the stove, didn't hear his grandson's greeting.

"Hey, Pap," McCabe yelled again, "Whatcha up to?"

Still holding the old wooden spoon he'd been using, the elder McCabe turned toward the door. A small, wiry man, he moved quickly to his grandson. The spoon clattered to the floor as the old man hugged him.

"You trying to scare me half to death, boy?" Joseph finally rasped. "Whatcha doing here on a Wednesday anyway?" Watery blue eyes stared out at McCabe. His grandfather's bony, worn features were unrelieved by any hint of a smile. "You know I'm happy enough to see you, Clinton, but I got a feeling something's wrong."

Smiling uncertainly, Clint McCabe reflected his grandfather's uneasiness. "Everything's fine, Pap. I just come home for a little vacation. City got too much for me."

"Vacation hell!" Joseph bawled over the urgent chanting of the gospel song. "You done quit your job, ain't you?" He rounded on his grandson. "Oh my God, Clinton, ain't you ever gonna amount to anything? I know the devil's got into your soul, boy. You're gonna burn in the fires, boy!"

By now old Joseph's ranting was even louder than the gospel music. The younger man stepped backward, away from his grandfather's fury. He'd known the old man was crazy, especially when he drank, but he hadn't expected this reception.

Joseph sat down heavily at the table, his meal forgotten on the stove. Weeping, he grasped the half full glass of whiskey at his elbow. "I done railroaded forty years," he mumbled. "Never missed a day. Give me a gold watch." He gulped the drink. "Done tried, Clinton. Done tried to raise you up right since your mama died. Prayed for you, boy."

"Hey, Pap," McCabe said over his shoulder as he left the room, "I won't be staying. Just come by to pick up a few things." He turned away from the look on Joseph's face. "Sorry, Pap, I just couldn't stand it down in D.C. Felt like I was caged up. Could you and me talk later?"

"You gonna burn in the fires, boy!" Pap's voice followed McCabe out of the kitchen.

Old McCabe was still weeping, the whiskey glass empty now, as his grandson quietly let himself out the front door. Dragging his old camping gear to the truck, McCabe wished things had gone better with the old man.

* * * *

A week later, McCabe was sitting by a fire on the shore of the Cacapon River. He looked across at the exhausted tourists huddled in small groups. The evening meal was over and most looked ready to turn in. Listening to the soft chords of the harmonicas, he decided that the Grayson brothers' version of "Sweet Baby James" wasn't bad. They were also members of the river guide crew, sent out by the local resort. John and Zeke Grayson had been working summers at the resort for years and had helped McCabe get the job. It had been a lucky break, as jobs were hard to find in Morgan County. He was sure he could count on at least three months of work, depending on the weather.

"I got a full house," Zeke Grayson drawled as he laid down the worn playing cards. The firelight played on the lean, tanned faces of the river crew as they concentrated on the game.

"Hell, you gonna clean me out, Grayson," McCabe groaned as he shoved over his pile of cash. He didn't really care if he lost a few bucks. It was damn relaxing to play a little poker with these guys at the end of the day.

"Hey McCabe," Grayson called from where he lounged against a pile of gear, "Hear you could hardly run fast enough to git away from that blonde tourist chasing you last week." John was grinning broadly. His shaggy red hair fell over his eyes, making it hard for McCabe to gauge his intent.

"Yeah, we hear she chased you through camp and all the way up the mountain," Zeke added. "She was yelling, 'Oh Clint, Clint, wait for me. I surely haven't seen all the sights you promised to show me yet!'" Zeke's voice took on a high-pitched, city accent.

"Oh my goodness, Clint," John continued in a lilting soprano, "the guide book promised I'd see Wild, Wonderful West Virginia, but you just keep running away!"

The rest of the men were whooping with laughter, stomping their feet, and shouting encouragement. Zeke was up on his tiptoes, twirling around the circle of the fire, lifting imaginary skirts high above his muddy sneakers. "Oh, Mr. McCabe," he moaned, "You are such an animal!"

Although McCabe turned bright red, he laughed along with the others. He'd been the butt of good-natured ribbing since he'd joined the group. He was the youngest of the crew and his dark good looks and lean, hard physique seemed to attract the ladies. There had been a few he'd thought were knockouts, but he'd been uneasy around them. The women he'd known so far had been direct and uncomplicated. These women were neither. Maybe it was their age, he thought. The women who could afford the 'Scenic Cacapon Cruise' were older—in their thirties. Usually they had successful careers and were used to dealing with men in an offhand, yet aggressive manner. They scared the hell out of him.

"Speaking of women," Zeke said. "Whatever happened to Lisa Marshall? Weren't you two together for a while?"

"Wish I knew," McCabe answered slowly. "I've called her a couple a times. She's always busy. Told me I should join the freaking army." He snorted. "I hear she's seeing some guy from Martinsburg. He's divorced, or so he says. You know that ain't gonna work out." He hoped his bitterness didn't show.

* * * *

Later that night, he was about to drift off to sleep when he heard the Grayson brothers talking softly. They must have thought that he was sleeping inside the tent. From the direction of their voices, McCabe figured they were still near the fire.

"McCabe's O.K., matter of fact I like the guy," John said, "but he sure as hell better git it together. Army, hell! He wouldn't last in the military, ain't the type."

"Soon as he got his first leave, they'd never see him again." Zeke agreed. "He'd lose hisself in these hills and that would be the end of him!"

"When they court-marshaled his ass, they'd call him Unfit for Military Life," John said.

"He asked me about helping him to git on driving school bus with you and me. But hell, John, soon as hunting season come, he'd take off for a week or two! He just ain't reliable."

"Well look at his family, Zeke. His daddy done run off and his Uncle Jason's still in jail. His cousin, Jake, drifts from job to job. Old Joseph is the best of the bunch, but since he's got religion, he's gone crazy—drinks like a fish since the old lady died."

"Yeah," Zeke said. Poor bastard ain't got a chance. He's a damn good worker though. Hope he hangs on 'til the end of August."

Well shit! McCabe eased his head back down on the pillow. A man seldom got to know what others really thought of him. He grinned. At least they agreed with him about the freaking army.

* * * *

A week later Jake McCabe's old Ford pickup rattled up to the evening campsite. He found his cousin setting up the big mess tent with two of the other crew workers.

"Need to see you a minute, Clint," Jake said.

One look at him told McCabe that something was wrong. Jake's usual jauntiness was gone. His dark eyes were somber. "It's the old man, ain't it?" McCabe asked.

Jake nodded. "Come to git you just in case," he said. "Pap ain't good. A neighbor lady found him last night. He'd had a stroke. He asked for you, Clint."

* * * *

Joseph McCabe died two days later. He has lapsed into a coma by the time his grandsons made it to the hospital. Clint McCabe was amazed at the overwhelming sense of loss he felt. His depression was only increased by the large amounts of booze he drank to get himself through the traditional McCabe family funeral and wake.

The whole county turned out. Old Joseph had known everybody. Uncle Jason was released from Regional Jail for the day of the funeral. No one was glad to see him. His son, Jake, was embarrassed. Jake and his young wife, Jan, smiled nervously at the pale, withdrawn stranger. The rest of the McCabe family ignored Jason entirely. Uncertain, but taking their cue from the family, friends and neighbors passed silently by Jason McCabe.

Clint McCabe would have been happy to be ignored by the mourners. He was actually sought out. Lisa came, teary eyed but distant, to murmur her condolences. The river guide crew, ill at ease in their dark suits, spoke quietly with him. Various relatives bore down on him, intent on offering sympathy and advice. McCabe wanted neither.

Finally escaping to the kitchen, he stopped short. He could see Pap there by the stove, wooden spoon raised in his hand like a weapon, fire in his eyes—eyes that accused his grandson. "You gonna burn in the fires, boy!" Old Joseph's voice followed McCabe out of the kitchen. Running over to his truck, he grabbed the bottle of whiskey he'd stashed there and headed towards the barn.

Although he spotted the police officer sent to guard Jason, McCabe was still surprised to find his uncle inside the barn. The two men stared at each other quietly for a while. Then McCabe handed Jason the bottle.

"You don't like this show no better than I do, do you?" McCabe asked.

"You don't fit in no better than I do, do you, boy? I been watching you." Jason said. He took a long swig from the bottle, but didn't return it. "You're a lot like your daddy, Clinton. Do you know that?" As Jason looked at his nephew, his eyes held a flat expression.

"Figured I must be," McCabe replied. "You know where he is?"

"Dead, probably, and better off too, I reckon." Jason took another shot from the bottle and handed it back. "Got to go now, Clinton. Remember, your grandpap was a powerful man once. Useta scare the shit outta me. But look at him now. Next it'll be our turn." Jason walked away. At the door he turned and said with conviction, "I'm sure we'll meet again, Clinton-somewhere." The barn door clattered shut behind him.

A vision of his uncle's pale, hopeless eyes lasted in McCabe's mind long after Jason had left. This image was sometimes replaced with Lisa's disappointed gaze. McCabe nursed the bottle of whiskey and remembered the good times with Pap. But unbidden, Pap's accusing words would tumble back into his thoughts. "You'll burn in the fires, boy! You'll burn!" When Jake finally found him, McCabe had passed out on the bales of hay.

* * * *

Although McCabe had been back at work with the river crew for several weeks, he couldn't shake his depression. He worked methodically, but didn't joke around anymore. The only relief he got was from the bottle he kept hidden in his gear. With only two more weeks left in the season, he began to worry about what he would do next. He'd saved very little of his pay. Between those trips to the local bars and the poker games, he hadn't had much left. Now, he had no home to return to. Pap's place had been taken by the bank and sold to cover his debts.

Every time the rafts passed by a big, fancy vacation house on shore, McCabe began to calculate how much the "take" would be. It'd be child's play to rip off the TVs, DVDs, guns, copper wire and other valuables and fence them in Martinsburg or Winchester. He wouldn't get rich, but he'd make out O.K., and at very little risk. Anyone who knew the river and hills could move in and out unnoticed. In the fall most places would be deserted. It'd be so easy. He smiled. He could do a little hunting, a little trapping. He'd get by.

Unbidden, Uncle Jason's pale face flashed before his eyes. "We'll meet again, somewhere," his uncle whispered. Jason had spent a lot of time taking things that weren't his, McCabe knew. But Jason had been a bungler and ended up a three-time loser. He was away for life. Hell! McCabe thought, he ain't the first local man to go to jail and he won't be he last. What am I so spooked about?

* * * *

It had sure been easier than he ever dreamed it would be, McCabe thought as he drew another "X" over a section of the Morgan County map. That last haul had netted a nice piece of change—enough to buy parts for the truck and some of the other good things in life. "Standard of living's improving," he said aloud. "Whole damn life's improving." Clint McCabe surveyed the compact trailer he had 'liberated' from a dealer's lot, hitched up to his truck and brought to this deserted mountain top. Guy will never miss this little beauty. I sure as hell need it more than he does, he thought.

He flipped on the large flat screen TV he had gotten from one of the fancy cabins near the power dam. It was brand new—really too big for this little trailer. Lucky he was able to jerry-rig the electric line up here from the pole on the ridge, or there'd be no TV, no fridge, nothing. Moving over to the small refrigerator, he pulled out a beer. Man, this was the life! Trying to prop his bare feet up on the nearby bunk, he knocked over a stack of boxed ammunition.

"Shit!" McCabe yelled. Looking around at the piles of DVD and CD players lining one wall, he mentally added up the number of firearms stashed under the bunks and groaned. He'd found an honest fence named Ernie down in Martinsburg. When Ernie was out of town, he had to use a dealer in Hancock. "Gotta git rid of this stuff soon. It's running me outta here," he muttered.

It had only been a month and he figured he'd done very well indeed. Hardly any risk. That was because he was smart, went about it scientific, like a business—which, of course, it was. A damn good business, and he was the boss! First he'd block off a section of the map in the summer resident area, then he'd methodically case each "hit." He always took his time, never rushed, so he knew just what to expect.

If it went good tonight, he promised himself, he'd retire for a couple weeks. He'd take it easy—hadn't even had no time to hunt—working too damn hard. McCabe flipped the channel selector. If he weren't lonely as hell, it'd be a great life.

* * * *

Working efficiently, McCabe had piled numerous items together. The full moon flooded the large, high-beamed room, illuminating the well stocked bar and the African-looking spears mounted over the massive stone fireplace. Them spears might be valuable to a collector, he noted. Pausing, he grabbed a couple of bottles of five-star cognac. Funny, he thought, he was sure them drapes was closed last night. Most people pull the curtains when they leave. But no car in the drive, no lights. No, nobody here—just mistaken.

The blow caught McCabe on the side of the head and sent him sprawling. Struggling into a sitting position, he looked into the barrel of a 30-30. His head throbbed. "Damn!" He said as he tried to wipe away the blood running down his cheek. The 30-30 swayed back and forth close to his temple. Holding it was a young, very pale, blond woman.

"Don't move!" she ordered in a high-pitched voice.

"Don't think I can. What the hell you hit me with, lady?"

"I said don't move, or I'll shoot you." She nodded her head in the direction of the steam iron lying on the floor near him. "Hit you with that iron. You deserved it!"

McCabe watched her. Not only was the rifle swaying— she was swaying. Her whole body moved in a slow circular movement. What the hell was wrong with her? She sounded funny too, slurring her words.

"Shit, Lady! You're drunker than a skunk!" he hooted.

As he watched, her eyes blinked shut and she slowly spiraled to the floor, rifle slipping from her grasp. McCabe struggled over to her. Shoving the rifle out of reach, he stared down at her. God! She was beautiful! Young, maybe his age—blond hair fell over her face. Her lips were full and slightly parted. "Damn! You smell like a brewery!" He recoiled.

Opening soft, dark eyes, she stared blankly at him. "Who are you?"

"Just your friendly neighborhood crook." He pulled a pile of small napkins from the bar and tried to mop up the blood. Hell, he must look awful. She was scared of him. No, too drunk to really be scared. Lucky blow she got in on him. How'd she do it?

Struggling to one elbow, she looked puzzled. "What are you doing here?" She demanded.

"There wasn't supposed to be nobody here, no car outside. How'd you git here?" McCabe got to his feet. "Here, git up."

Meekly she allowed herself to be propped up in a chair, although she kept slumping and her eyes kept closing. Suddenly her head shot up and her eyes blinked wide open. "My car quit on me about 500 feet up the driveway. No luck—no luck in my life. Uncle Louie didn't leave any food here, only booze." Her eyes shut again.

McCabe looked at her. She wore a T-shirt and tight-fitting jeans. Damn good set of knockers, small waist, long legs— beautiful. And look at me, covered with blood and here robbing her house—her uncle's house. And she thinks SHE don't have no luck! Shit!

"Don't even like the stuff," she mumbled. "Roger always said I was a cheap drunk. Never drank before I married him... son-of-a-bitch!" She started moving convulsively and held her stomach. "Get me a bowl, a towel, something, quick!"

"Christ, you're gonna puke, ain't you?" He ran toward the kitchen, clutching his head with one hand. Grabbing a pot and a roll of paper towels, he raced back to the girl. Her face had turned gray and she was gagging. Shoving the stuff at her, he realized how ironic the whole damn mess was. Dreamed of a woman like her. Christ, look at her! Look at me! He started laughing. He laughed until he had to sit down.

"Ain't neither one of us ever had no luck. Shit! What a pair we make!" The throbbing in his head finally quieted him. Gotta git out of here. What am I doing? He thought as he staggered to his feet and moved unsteadily toward the door.

"Help!" Her voice broke his stride. "You can't leave me like this."

"Can't leave you! Lady, are you crazy? You oughta be glad I'm leaving. I just tried to rob you."

"Well, then you owe me."

"You're crazy. I'm gettin' outta here." He reached the door.

"I think I'm going to be sick again. Oh God," she moaned. "If I could just make it to the bed."

McCabe's hand was on the door handle. He turned in time to see her heave herself out of the chair and fall flat on the floor. She started to groan. That did it! Cursing under his breath he headed back toward her. "C'mon," he mumbled as he half dragged, half carried her down the hall. She landed on the bed like a sack of potatoes and stared up at him.

"You O.K.?" He asked tentatively.

"No, I'm not O.K.." Tears began to well from the dark eyes. "No car, no money, no food." She paused to wipe at the tears. "No husband, no job, 300 miles from home—stuck in this, this wilderness! Not O.K. at all." Her eyelids fluttered closed, but the soft sobbing continued.

"Look, would you like a cup of coffee of something?" McCabe shifted uncomfortably. His head was throbbing. He had to get out of here!

She didn't answer. He edged nearer the door. "Wait!" she tried to raise her head. "Oh, my head!" She groaned.

"Your head! What about my head? You tried to kill me!" he shouted at her. "What do you want from me?"

"You scared me half to death, sneaking around like that! It's your fault, not mine. Now you owe me!" Her head sank back on the pillow.

"Owe you!" he snorted. "You really are crazy! It's not my fault you got yourself sloshed, or your car broke down, or your old man left you, or any of the rest of it!"

"I left him, the son-of-a-bitch!" she retorted, then meekly asked, "Could you please get me a Coke? It would settle my stomach."

"Sure, be right back." McCabe ran for the door. On the way out he picked up the phone. As he had hoped, it was dead. But the girl probably had a cell phone and she could positively I.D. him. Sooner or later, she would.

A few minutes later he reached the Jon boat he'd left at the dock. Crazy girl! Asking the local thief to put her to bed! Even drunk as she was, it was a very dangerous thing to do. But as he pulled out into the current, the image of her dark, tear-filled eyes followed him. "Damn!" He shouted, "Don't never have no damn luck!"

Five hours later, just as the dawn was breaking over the purple mountain ridges, McCabe found himself back at the same dock. "Fool!" He muttered, "You're nothing but a damn fool!" Grabbing a sack of groceries and a small toolbox, he walked cautiously toward the house. Circling back to the bed-rooms, he identified the window of the room where he'd left the girl. She was still there, sprawled on the bed, her blond hair spread out around her. Wish things had been different, he thought.

He found the blue Honda with New Jersey plates halfway up the long drive and ended up working about two hours. Thank God he hadn't needed any parts! Before he left he scribbled a note on the back of an envelope, "From one loser to another, hope your luck turns." As he left the note on the front seat, his eye fell on a copy of the Morgan Messenger. The banner headline read, 'Vacationland Bandit Strikes

Again.' Just upset her to read this, McCabe reasoned as he took the newspaper.

* * * *

For the next two weeks he purposely stayed away from that section of the river. He was busy enough hunting by day and thieving by night. What a great life, he thought—plenty of money. Not a problem in the world! According to town gossip and the local papers, the 'State Boys' didn't have a clue. Yeah, things were great, McCabe kept telling himself. Every time he unloaded down in Martinsburg, he hit his favorite bars. Through his fence, Ernie, he had met a very friendly and experienced woman named Diane. She got off on sex and money—not necessarily in that order. So what was the problem?

The problem was that most nights he couldn't sleep at all. The blonde girl kept invading every dream. Her long hair was falling over his chest, her long legs entwined with his. Christ, he couldn't stand it! The more time he spent with Diane in Martinsburg, the hornier he got. It wasn't supposed to work that way!

Finally, one cold, misty evening in mid-October, he deliberately picked up a pair of binoculars acquired the previous night. Silently, he moved through the woods to a high bluff overlooking her house—her uncle's house.

"Yeah," he grunted, "car's still there. Thought she might be back in New Jersey by now—back to civilization." But no, he noticed a thin spiral of smoke rising from the stone chimney. Then his gaze shifted to what looked like and old sheet hanging between the flagpole and a pine tree. Squinting, he read the message printed in big red letters, "HEY, LOSER—COME TO DINNER—6 P.M.

"Now I know that woman's crazy!" But McCabe grinned and started back toward the trailer at a fast trot. Well, she just may be crazy, he thought, but she sure don't know how crazy the McCabes are!

* * * *

Twenty minutes later he landed the boat some distance downstream and made his way carefully to a spot behind the house. After about a half an hour of watching and listening, he slid in through one of the rear windows. He made out the sound of guitar music—not anything he recognized, definitely not 'country.' When he was sure she was alone, he walked into the living room and sat down on the couch. He could hear her in the kitchen. "Hey, honey," he shouted over the guitar beat. "It's past six, where's dinner?"

She bolted out of the kitchen, a pot raised defensively. Eyes round with surprise, she gaped at him.

"How did you get in here?"

"Same way I did before, but this time I was invited." He grinned at her. She looked even better than he remembered.

"How about getting those muddy boots off the coffee table, Mister ah, Mister…?"

"McCabe," he filled in helpfully. "Sorry ma'am, just habit." He quickly got to his feet. With a flourish he handed her the paper wrapped package he'd brought with him. "Us McCabes don't accept no invitations without bringing something along."

"Funny, I thought you McCabes usually left with something instead!" She grinned back at him. Her hand brushed his as she took the soggy package. "What's in it?" she asked suspiciously. "And why can't you come to the door like a normal person?"

He blinked. "It's squirrel, ma'am. Best damn thing in the world if you bread it and fry it up, make a little gravy. Tastes like chicken."

"Squirrel! I know nothing about cooking squirrel. And the name is Allison, Allison Martin, Mr. McCabe."

"No, not 'Mr. McCabe', just McCabe. That's what everybody calls me." He was beginning to feel uncomfortable.

"Some idea you had about the message out there on that ol' sheet."

"Well, I just wanted to thank you properly. You were very kind—fixing the car and leaving that bag of food. I wasn't sure when you'd see the invitation, but that didn't matter. I can always whip up something. Don't worry, I never reported anything," she added quickly. "And I, well…I guess I hit you pretty hard."

"Oh, I'm healing up good, don't you… Shit! The damn squirrel's leaking!" He scrambled to scoop up the sticky, dark blood that dripped onto the cream-colored carpet. "Sorry, Ma'am…er, Allison. I didn't realize the squirrel was…I mean…do you have a rag, or something?"

She raced toward the kitchen like a woman chased by demons. "It's all over my white sneakers," he heard her moan.

Well, what else can I expect, he asked himself. She's horrified, disgusted, thinks I'm a caveman or something. Christ! I've really screwed this one up!

During the promised 'thank you dinner', Allison kept up polite chatter. McCabe ate silently. The food was terrible! No gravy, no biscuits, terrible! Thank God her uncle kept a well-stocked bar. She'd tried to talk him into wine with dinner, but he said he never touched the stuff. He took a long swallow of whiskey. She said she wasn't much of a drinker—not her style—no matter what idea he may have gotten about her. Well, maybe, he thought. How should he know? She was drinking Coke with her dinner. He tried to focus on her words instead of her full lips.

"So I'm officially on the substitute list at the area schools now," she was saying. "I've worked three days in a row and I can see why they can't keep subs!" Her voice trailed off as she watched him.

Beautiful girl, he was thinking. Bet she would be something else in the sack. After all, she has been married…how long did she say…almost a year. Well shit! Oughta be broke in by now! He studied her from under half-closed eyelids and smiled.

"Mr. McCabe!" She said sharply and glared at him. "I'm not one of the items on the menu! I don't think you've heard a thing I've said."

"Why. Yes I have, really. And I'm real happy things are working out for you." He tried to sound as polite and 'civilized' as possible. "Actually, I've been thinking about you and wondering how you was getting along all alone here." Man, that was no kidding!

"The food is real good, wonderful!" He tried to smile convincingly. Whole thing's crazy, he thought. Two weeks ago I was trying to rob her and she was drunker than a skunk! Now look at us—acting like we was in a high-class restaurant—only the food would have to be better!

Looking around at the collection of what he guessed was some kind of African or native art hanging on the walls, he said, "Very interesting art work. Is your uncle one of them collectors?"

"Well, no, not a collector really. You see, my family serve as missionaries. They've traveled all over the world. That's why Uncle Louie has all these pieces. They were mainly gifts from my parents. Uncle Louie wanted to be a missionary too, but he has always had a weak heart. He had to go into banking," she said apologetically.

"I guess a lot of people can't really do what they want in life. Like you and me, for instance. Things haven't worked out very well for either one of us, have they?" She smiled at him. "Have you ever thought about what you're going to do with your life?"

"Well, ah, no, not much. I guess things are pretty messed up." Man! He had to get her off this subject. If she thought about it much more, she'd probably throw him out! "So your family's in the missionary line?" he asked.

She brightened. "Oh yes, my parents have been in India for two years now. I miss them, but they are very happy there."

She seemed real fired up. I'm on the right track now, Mc-Cabe thought. Don't was to piss her off no more if I can help it. He nodded earnestly.

"And my brother, Jim, is on his first assignment down in Columbia, South America," she continued. "He's only been there for a couple of weeks. I did get a chance to see him right before he left. When he found out I was here, he stopped by. I've been trying to get in touch with him to see how things are going down there."

"Must be an interesting life. Have you ever felt like breaking loose and heading to the jungles to save them heathens?"

"Well, actually, yes. That's one reason I'm trying to get in touch with my brother." Her eyes lit up and she spoke excitedly. "They need teachers there and, well, I've made a mess of things here. Yes, I am thinking about it."

"What about your husband?" he asked cautiously. "He let you go?"

"Let me go!" she snorted. "I'd like to see him try to stop me! I filed the divorce papers yesterday. It may take a while, but that's okay. Actually, things had not been too good between us for a while, then I caught him in bed with my best friend," she said hotly. "I don't ever want to see Roger Martin again. I'm going to take back my maiden name, too—Whitehead. I'll be Allison Whitehead again."

"Yeah, I remember Roger, that sonuvabitch!" McCabe grinned at her. "He musta been some kinda damn fool!"

She grinned back. "Are you still up to your evil ways, McCabe?"

He shifted uncomfortable. Shit! Why did her family all have to be preachers? No damn luck at all. He knew what was coming now. "Ah, well…" he began awkwardly.

"Never mind!" She cut him off. "I've been following your career in the newspapers. You're just building up more debt, that's all."

"Debt?" he shouted. "Debt! Like I owe somebody? What in the world are you talking about?"

"This isn't the right time to discuss it," she replied calmly. "By the way, why did it take you so long, McCabe?"

She was a damn complicated woman. "Take me so long?"

"I put that banner up out front over two weeks ago. Where were you?" she asked seriously. "After all, you knew you were the only person I had, ah, met in this wilderness. Yes, where were you?"

"Where was I? Man! If you only knew, Allison." He grinned, hoping he was avoiding that look she didn't seem to like. "If you need some help, send me a signal. Put something red on the flagpole. I'll be here."

* * * *

Again, McCabe thought he ought to do himself a big favor and stay far away from Allison. In the first place, she was crazy. In the second place, she was so damn complicated that half the time he couldn't figure her out at all. She went to a lot of trouble to invite him to dinner and assure him that she hadn't turned him in. He believed her. But then she told him that he owed a debt to somebody. She didn't say who he owed, or why. Then she asked him what he planned to do with his life. What kinda question was that?

She was built like a brick shit-house and dressed in tight jeans that made her body look great, but she didn't like the way he looked at her! Hell! How was a man supposed to look at her? She was not only the most beautiful girl he'd ever known, she was also the most tormenting. She wasn't like any of the women he'd ever known before. They often said one thing and meant another, but it was usually, "No, NO!" while they helped him with their blouse buttons! Yeah, the more he thought about Allison, the more confused he got.

* * * *

McCabe spent a day sectioning up the meat from three fat white-tailed does. No sense waiting for the season to start, he reasoned. Then they'd be so gun-shy, he never would've been able to bag these here tender little beauties! He knew he'd have to get all the deer meat packed away in Jake's chest freezer by that evening. Jake was always glad to see him, as most of the meat would end up on Jake and Jan's dinner table. Yeah, Jake was O.K.. It was Jan who worried McCabe. He thought she didn't look too happy to see him these days. Didn't seem to want him hanging around with Jake no more, neither. Matter of fact, the last time he'd seen her, she'd looked at him like he was an ax murderer!

As he was packing the boxes of deer meat into the pickup, McCabe thought about taking a package over to Allison. Shit! He was always thinking about Allison. Then he remembered the leaking squirrel mess and her cool response.

He tried to picture Diane in the same situation. This wasn't easy because Diane could turn out some mean fried squirrel. But anyway, if Diane had been pissed at him, the whole world would have known it. No polite but icy: "I know nothing about cooking squirrel, Mr. McCabe." Diane would have thrown the squirrel back in his face and said, "Take your damn shit outta here, McCabe, you sonuvabitch!" And then she'd have probably tried to backhand him! He grinned. That reaction he could understand!

* * * *

Using the binoculars, he had checked Allison's place every evening for the last few weeks. Nothing. But today an old red T-shirt fluttered from the flagpole. McCabe smiled. And this time he was sure it was the smile she didn't like. He was going to see her again!

She ain't gonna turn me over to the cops, he told himself as he circled the house. She would've already done it by now. Still, he checked things out. Finally, he walked up to the front door and knocked.

"McCabe," Allison said as she opened the door, "I'm glad you're here. Come in!"

There she goes, he thought as he stepped through the door. She's saying one thing, but probably meaning another. This sure ain't no glad type greeting! Aloud, he said, "Hi. You O.K.?"

"I'm doing fine. No problems. That's what I wanted to tell you." She looked relaxed, and yeah, she looked happy. Not so bitchy. This was very good!

"Great!" He tried to sound casual. "I've been wondering how you was getting along. You look, ah, good."

She shot him a sidelong glance. "I did have a couple of reasons for getting in touch, for one thing, I've heard from my brother, Jim."

"Still saving souls in the jungle, is he? Ain't ended up in no cooking pot yet?"

Allison rolled her eyes. "He just sent me a video from the mission. And I thought since you were one of the few people I, ah, knew here, you might want to watch it with me."

Woman has no sense of humor. Looks like I pissed her off again. Well hell! What am I supposed to say? I don't give a shit about her brother. He said, "Just kidding! Sure, I'd like to see the video."

Allison busied herself with the DVD. "The police were here yesterday," she said. "They were checking with all the residents in the area. They wanted to know if I'd seen or heard anything out-of-the-ordinary. One of the officers said it could be dangerous for me here alone." She grinned up at him. "But then, I already know that, don't I."

McCabe grinned back. He wasn't surprised that the cops were checking up. Finally doing their jobs—lazy bastards. Fat lota good it'd do 'em! "Don't worry about the cops," he said confidently.

"Un huh. Well, for your sake I hope you're right. Get yourself a drink, McCabe." She gestured toward the coffee table. "I made some whole wheat sandwiches if you're hungry."

McCabe looked over the food without much hope. At least her uncle's booze was first class.

The video, shot from a plane, panned over blue mountain ridges. The silver thread of a river ran through the valley. "My God!" McCabe said, "Looks like West Virginia. Beautiful!"

"It sure is!" Allison agreed. "Jim said in his letter that these next scenes of the Indian village were shot from a jeep on the day he arrived."

Small groups of smiling Indians ran after the jeep. A few shabby wooden structures bounced into view, but most of the homes were small, rounded huts. Now the jungle closed in around the jeep. "Look, McCabe, a monkey!" Allison said.

He picked out the small creature jumping around excitedly on a high tree limb. The jeep must have slowed down, as the focus improved. Allison was watching him expectantly.

"Cute little fella," McCabe said. Don't look like there's much meat to fry up on that bugger, he concluded silently. No wonder them Indians all looked so scrawny. McCabe eyed the dense vegetation with interest. What would the hunting be like? Man would need to make hisself a tree stand and wear camouflage. That'd be the thing to do. Probably be hot as hell.

"Now there're entering the mission compound," Allison explained. Several dingy white frame buildings clustered around a larger building, which was topped with a cross. Orange dust seemed to cover everything. Distant mountain ridges loomed over the hillside mission.

The jeep bumped to a stop and the screen went blank. Then the camera steadied and focused on a tall young man walking toward the church. He stopped, turned and smiled broadly at the camera. Groups of skinny children were running toward him.

"That's Jim. The kids are from the mission school," Allison said. "It is so great to see him there. Wait until you hear him preach his first sermon—that's at the end of the video. He's a fantastic speaker. The Indians love him!"

Oh Christ! McCabe groaned inwardly—a sermon! He'd heard all the preaching he'd ever wanted to hear when he'd been dragged to church by Grandpap! He took a big gulp of whiskey.

Dressed in clerical robes, the Reverend Jim Whitehead smiled down at his congregation. "Brothers and Sisters," he began. "You are all children of the Lord. He watches over you. His love is all around you and his mercy is all-forgiving. Even those of you who have been sinners can once again walk in the light of His love!" He paused, but wasn't smiling. Man! He's got 'em squirming, McCabe thought. They must know what's coming!

"How many of you have strayed from the path of the righteous?" Jim demanded. "How many have taken what wasn't theirs?" He stopped again, his stern gaze travelling around the church. Several of the men lowered their heads. "How many have looked with desire on their neighbor's wives? How many have lusted in their hearts? How many have committed adultery?" Jim's voice grew louder, sterner. His eyes moved slowly from face to face. This accusation was met with shuffling and faint coughing noises. The camera panned over the congregation, catching their uneasy glances and averted black eyes.

Poor bastards! Well, every one of 'em is a damn sinner and he knows it. Just like in West Virginia, McCabe decided. Shit! He's even got me squirming—all that talk about stealing and lusting. He glanced over at Allison, who was watching the screen intently.

"Isn't he wonderful?" She said. "In the letter he explained that there had been an explosion of moral problems just before he arrived. The mission had been without a minister for several months."

"He's sure setting them poor devils straight. Puts me in mind of my Grandpap," McCabe said.

"I'm so proud of him," Allison was saying. "I really look up to him, putting up with all the hardships just to help those people."

"Yeah," McCabe agreed. "Hardships."

"Oh yes, he writes that there's never enough money to do what needs to be done. The crops fail. Diseases cause many deaths among the Indians. There're never enough medical supplies." But instead of looking saddened by this list of woes, McCabe thought she looked, well not exactly happy, but definitely fired up.

"There's so much to do." She looked at him intently. "I can't wait to get there!"

"Git there?"

"Well, I'm trying to work things out. I could really be useful there. I applied for my visa weeks ago."

McCabe couldn't believe it. She was really leaving? Going to some hole in the jungle to work herself to death—and for what?

"That's it," Allison said as the screen went blank. "What did you think of Jim?"

"He sure does some powerful preaching. Bet he has all them sinning Indians whipped into shape by now!" She smiled at this. He noticed that her eyes took on an almost hazel shade when she was happy. Damn, now she was talking about leaving. Just his shitty luck!

"You seem like a man of many talents, McCabe. Just what type of work did you do before, ah…before now?"

"Actually, I can turn my hand at just about anything," he drawled. "Last summer I worked with a river crew dragging tourists down river. Before that I worked construction in the city. I've done a little electrical work," he finished, thinking of the jerry-rigged line to his trailer.

"Mmmm, Jack-of-all-trades," she murmured. McCabe thought her eyes took on a calculating look. "With all that talent, you could still be…I mean, you could still lead a very useful life if the right opportunity came along."

"What's that?" He said, suddenly alerted. The sound of a car engine drew nearer. Tires crunched over the gravel driveway.

Allison ran to the window. "It's the police car again!" Panic made her voice shrill. "Quick, hide in the back bedroom."

Well, this is it, McCabe thought. She's done turned me in. Could all this have been a trap?

"Yes, Officer." He heard Allison's voice clearly from his hiding place. "Everything is fine, no problems." He eased his breath out in relief. "No, it's not necessary to check on me every night. I know you're very busy."

McCabe couldn't pick up the low response. He was pretty sure there was only one cop in the house. He edged to the window. The patrol car looked empty. Of course, the guy's partner could be sneaking around outside right now. He didn't know whether it was riskier to go or to stay.

Undecided, he listened to Allison. "No, really I'm not afraid to be here alone. I'm used to the place by now."

Carefully, he leaned around the doorframe. Allison had her back to him, but he could see the cop clearly. Something about the way he's standing there bothers me, McCabe thought. For one thing, he's standing much too close to Allison. He was able to catch the cop's next words.

"You see, ma'am, I just never would forgive myself if anything happened to a pretty young girl like you. It's no bother stopping by." His voice was smooth and deep.

McCabe stiffened. "Damn bastard," he swore under his breath. "He's putting a move on her." Protection of the law, HA! Well, at least he knew HE was safe. This here cop wasn't interested in catching crooks tonight. Sonuvabitch should hear one a Reverend Jim's sermons! Probably got a wife and five kids at home. McCabe realized that his fists were clenched and the pulse in his neck was throbbing. He'd deck the guy if he laid a hand on Allison, cop or no cop!

He heard the front door slam shut and saw Allison racing toward him. "It's O.K., he's gone," she said jerkily. "But you've got to go! It's not safe for you here anymore!"

He wanted to reach out and comfort her, but he sensed this wasn't the right time. She looked very jumpy and scared now. Hell, there was never no right time!

She was hurrying him along the hall toward the back door.

"I'll be gone for a week or so." She spoke in short, out-of-breath gasps. "I've got to collect my belongings in New Jersey and settle things there. Maybe the law will give up on me if I'm not around for a while. Take care," she said while pushing him through the door and slamming it behind him.

McCabe got in a quick, "You too," before the door shut. He stood there in the silence. Would he ever see her again?

* * * *

The next morning McCabe awoke groggy and depressed. Never shoulda finished off that bottle of 'Beam' last night, he told himself. Big mistake!

While he shaved, he examined his lean, dark features in the mirror. With quick strokes, he shaved off the moustache he had just painstakingly grown. "Man, you gotta change more than that there moustache if you're gonna git anywheres with the lady," he said aloud. "You're gonna have to change your whole damn life! Look at you, you're a loser!"

Yeah, a loser. Couldn't work in the city. Couldn't work in the hills neither. Nothing suited him. So look at him now. "You're a damn crook, boy! You are a renegade from the law!" he shouted. "Every cop for miles 'round is hunting you. Sooner or later they'll git you. So you go and get hooked on a preacher's girl. You are one dumb ass!"

But Allison, what kinda man did she look up to? He already knew, her brother, Jim,—that's who. The preacher. By now he was pacing up and down in the confined space. His chances of following in the footsteps of brother Jim were about as good as a snowball's in hell.

* * * *

Later that night, McCabe was gathering up a hoard of guns and ammo in a cabin near Spruce Pine Hollow. He'd had to use the truck, but a least this place was on the way to Ernie's in Martinsburg. Just as he was getting ready to drag the haul boldly out the front door, he saw headlights flash in the driveway.

Shit! It was one thirty on a Wednesday night. What was this fool doing coming here now? He dropped the stuff and stumbled toward the rear of the house. Had to get outta there! The front door was opening as he slid through a back window. Glancing over his shoulder, he saw lights blaze on and heard the guy yelling. His pulse was racing by the time he made it back to where he'd left the pickup. Man! What shitty luck! That was the closest call he'd ever had! That is, he corrected himself, after Allison.

* * * *

The next day McCabe spent his time in Martinsburg bars. But the drinking didn't seem to help. He didn't even feel like seeing Diane. That close call in the cabin must have rattled him more than he'd realized. Well, he better look up Ernie and collect the money he had coming to him. Funny, he hadn't been able to get Ernie on the phone all day.

Just as he was paying up the bar bill, his cousin, Jake, walked in. "Hey, man, over here," McCabe shouted a greeting.

"Been looking for you," Jake said as he sat down.

"Good to see you, Jake," McCabe said. "What's up?"

"Git me a Bud," Jake hollered at the bargirl. He leaned back in the chair, but sure as hell didn't look relaxed. "I'm glad I found you, Clint. This here's the thing," he sat forward, looking uneasy. "Well, the cops been by the house a couple of times. It's like they're on to something. They're asking questions—about you, Clint." Jake took a long pull from the beer mug. "Seems your buddy, Ernie, took a fall. He's not the type to turn state's evidence, is he?" A nervous grin belied the fear in Jake's eyes.

"Hell, I don't know," McCabe said. "Anything's possible." He almost said, how do you think your dad was sent up the last time? The whole family knew that Jason McCabe had been fingered by his best pal when he'd been indicted. So now he was a habitual criminal, in for life.

"Well, I just wanted you to know," Jake got up to leave. "Guess you better not come around the house no more, Clint," he said hesitantly. "It ain't a good idea. Take care of yourself." Jake walked quickly toward the door.

Damn if that don't beat all, McCabe thought. Jake's my closest relative and just about my only friend. So much for friendship! That wife of his is probably behind this, he concluded.

* * * *

It rained heavily for the next few days and McCabe spent his time in the trailer. When he was drinking, which was most of the time, he thought about Allison—about the kinda man she would want, the kinda man she could love. It sure as hell wasn't him. But he could change. Hell, yes! No more thieving—that wasn't working out too good anyway. No more cussing. No more drinking. No more chewing tobacco. No more smart-ass remarks.

He decided that from now on he'd concentrate on polite conversation, like "Why, yes, I certainly enjoyed the evening." He tried out the words a couple of times—no bad grammar, keep it real smooth. "The meal was delicious. So very kind of you to invite me." He smiled, but tried to keep his expression cool.

McCabe went over the phrases a few more times, trying out the gestures and expressions he'd seen Jim use on the video. After a few more shots of 'Beam', he thought he was doing pretty good. He smiled without showing his teeth, the way the tourists on the river tour had done. He kept his voice low and soft. "I'm so delighted you were able to stop by," he intoned slowly.

"Yes!" He hooted. "I done got it now! If Allison wants a new, improved McCabe—she's got him!" Turning up the country beat on the radio, he two-stepped into the kitchen to find a new bottle of Jim Beam. Holding up the shot glass, he said, "To Preacher Jim. You see before you, Jim, a changed man!"

When he came down off the drunk, McCabe brooded over the mess he was in. Ernie was gonna talk sooner or later—if he hadn't already. But Ernie didn't know where he was. Only Jake knew. And if Jake knew, Jan knew. Well, he was safe until somebody offered a reward. Jan was a greedy little bitch. She'd wait until then.

During his waking hours, McCabe tried to reason things out calmly. But when he slept, he always dreamed the same dream. The gates of Regional Jail were opening, and Uncle Jason was waiting there to greet him. He awoke in a cold sweat. By the end of the week McCabe had come to a decision. He'd have to leave Morgan County—the thing he had never wanted to do. But he couldn't go without seeing Allison again.

* * * *

The next morning dawned clear and mild, a freak kind of day that sometimes came to the hills in November. Moving to the lookout, McCabe spotted the red cloth waving from Allison's flagpole. She was back and she wanted to see him. This was great! Fifteen minutes later, he was at her front door. The door jerked open and she almost dragged him inside.

"McCabe!" she said. "Thank God you're all right!" Grabbing up the local newspaper from atop a pile of luggage, she shoved it at him. "Look at the headline."

VICTIM OFFERS $1000 REWARD FOR BANDIT!

McCabe read the words slowly. Well, this was it. He was as good as behind bars as soon as Jan McCabe saw this. Too risky to go back to the trailer for anything now—time was out!

"Well, actually, I'd already decided to change my evil ways, starting about now," he said. "I'm glad you're back, Allison. I wanted to say good bye."

"Good bye? Where are you going to go? Where can you go?" She seemed alarmed. "Where will you be safe? Who will help you?"

"No idea," he answered, smiling at her. "But it sure is good to see you again." Could it be possible that she was really concerned for him?

"Sit down, McCabe," she ordered. "We need to talk." They sat facing each other across the kitchen table. "Listen, I'm flying out of Baltimore-Washington International Airport tonight—for Columbia, South America—for Jim's mission. I finally got all my papers in order." She paused; her dark eyes studied him as if she was trying to fit things together. "Do you want to come with me?" she asked. "You're a Jack of all Trades. You could be very useful there. It's the break you need. How about it?"

"How about it!" he whooped. "Lady, you got yourself a traveling companion!" He grabbed her face across the table and planted a quick, but solid kiss on her lips. "Just to seal the bargain." He grinned at her. She must like him a little bit. Shit! That was enough for him.

"Just to seal the bargain," she said, but she grinned.

"Wait a minute," he said slowly. He'd known this was too good to be true. "What about the airline ticket? And I don't have no passport or nothing—not much money. How can I…"

Allison cut him off. "We could pull it off if you wouldn't mind traveling as the Reverend James Whitehead. He left some of his clothes here, but the best thing is that his passport, visa, ticket, everything is right here!" She looked elated. McCabe shot her a puzzled look.

"You see," she continued, "Jim thought he had lost all of his papers and his ticket. We looked everywhere, but he finally had to get duplicates at the last minute. The Church Board helped him. They put the pressure on and rushed everything through."

She stopped to smile encouragingly, as though all this was too much to be believed. "Anyway, I found all the original papers a couple of weeks ago. They had fallen behind a slat in an old dresser drawer. I've checked the dates and everything is still good. What do you think?"

"I think it's the craziest damn scheme I've ever heard! How can I pass for Jim? What about his passport picture, for one thing?"

Allison pulled a pile of papers from the kitchen drawer. "Here's Jim's passport photograph." A dark-eyed, dark-haired, handsome young man stared back at them. She looked carefully at McCabe. "It's not impossible," she concluded. "Jim is about your age, and about your height and weight. It's a good thing you shaved off that moustache, although it did look good."

"You thought it looked good?" McCabe was unreasonably happy. Maybe, just maybe, his luck was beginning to turn.

"You'd need to wear a hat, maybe dark glasses, and—yes, I've got it!" She got up and ran out of the room. In a few minutes she returned with a high, round clerical collar. "This will do it, for sure!" she said triumphantly.

Thirty minutes later Allison was racing through the house closing everything down. "Hey, McCabe, could you check the window locks in the back of the house?" She called as she tried doors and checked locks in the huge living area. "We should get started."

"Sure thing," he answered. "Wouldn't want no real crook to git in!"

"Oh my God, McCabe!" he heard Allison wail. "It's that policeman again. Stay back there. I'll get rid of him."

He heard a car door slam. Well, if you think something's too good to be true, then it's too good to be true, he thought sadly. They were so close!

"Yes, Ma'am," he heard the deep-voiced cop say, "we have reason to believe he may be in your area." McCabe couldn't make out Allison's low reply. "So you're leaving then—Washington, D.C.? Mighty dangerous down there in the city. You take care!"

McCabe moved closer. "Yes, today, soon," Allison said. "My brother, er, the Reverend, and I are going to serve at a church center. So, I guess I'll never know whether you catch this guy or not. Well, good luck, Officer Rollins."

"Ah, Ma'am, hold on a minute." Oh shit, McCabe moaned. "Since you all are leaving," the cop continued, "you wouldn't mind if we set up our command post here in your driveway, would you? It's kinda a central location."

There was a long silence. "Of course not, Officer," Allison finally said. McCabe took one last look in the bedroom mirror. Yeah, he'd have to do. Adjusting the tight, round, clerical collar, he slammed the borrowed leather bush hat down on his head. The dark suit was a pretty good fit.

He walked confidently down the hall. "Guess we had better load the car, Sis," he said loudly, nodding to the cop as he carefully picked up several of the waiting suitcases.

"Have a good trip, Reverend," the cop said as McCabe strode out to the car. Allison followed with the remaining luggage. She looked nervous as hell. He knew that they better get out quick.

"Thank you, Officer, that's very kind of you." McCabe smiled his practiced, cool, tight-lipped smile. "My sister tells me you've had some problems here. I wish you the best of luck." He smiled again. "Oh, and thank you so much for looking in on my sister so often during this, ah, this crisis." He shot the cop a hard look. Lecherous bastard!

Leaning over, McCabe carefully placed the luggage in the trunk. Then, taking his time, he bent down and brushed a thin coating of dust from his boots. Waving in what he hoped was a friendly manner, he got into the driver's seat and slowly pulled away up the drive.

Puzzled, the cop looked after the departing car. Something bothered him about that guy, that preacher. About twenty minutes later, his backup arrived.

"Where's the good-looking woman you was bragging about, Rollins?" the second cop asked.

"She just left with her brother, the Reverend. She's moved out." He looked at his fellow officer uneasily. Something was still bothering him about the couple, about the preacher. "Where's this McCabe supposed to be now?" he asked.

According to the informant, he's somewhere in this here immediate area. But hell, sonuvabitch could be anywheres."

Officer Rollins pounded his fist down on the hood of the patrol car. "He ain't just anywheres. I'll bet you a month's pay he's on his way to Washington, D.C. with that poor, scared girl as his hostage. Reverend, my ass!" His face had turned crimson.

"Now I know what was wrong with the guy!" Rollins wagged his finger at the other cop. "In the first place, how many reverends wear hand-tooled cowboy boots? Eh? Answer me that! And all that fancy talk of his still couldn't cover up his 'twang.' Yeah, you just don't pick that up! It's bred in the bone! That bastard!

"And in the second place," Rollins continued, "how many preachers swagger around with a can a Skoal in their back pockets? That's the clincher! When he leaned over to put the luggage in the trunk, I'm real sure I saw the round outline of a Skoal can—you know it's real hard to mistake. Fancy preacher's suit and all, but damn if he wasn't carrying chewing tobacco. Cocky sonuvabitch too! Mean look in his eye. He ain't no reverend!"

The other officer was already on the car radio, "He'll never make it over the state line," he said. "A road bock should do it!"

"I bet he's heading for the Potomac River Bridge at Hancock and I-70. It's the fastest way to D.C.," Rollins said. "That's where we'll nab him."

* * * *

"Yaa-hooo!" McCabe shouted as he turned the Honda onto the hard-topped road and headed toward town. "We done done it, baby!" Reaching over, he slapped Allison's knee. "We're home free. Dumb-ass cop don't know which end is up!"

Shakily, Allison nodded. "You laid it on a little thick, didn't you, Reverend?" McCabe grinned the old grin, totally pleased with himself.

As they neared Hancock, he begin to worry. If, just if, something went really wrong, the bridge might be checked. Better not chance it. He swung the car off Route 522 onto Sand Mine Road. This way he could take back roads over to the Potomac River and check things out.

Fifteen minutes later, he edged the car along a narrow path near the Potomac. "Wait here, be right back," he told Allison. "Damn! Cops crawling all over the bridge," McCabe growled as he peered upriver from his vantage point on the shore. Well, they only had one choice now. And he'd thought his luck had turned!

He hurried back to the car. "Better change them high-heeled shoes," he told Allison. "We got some boating to do."

Quickly, they loaded the luggage in the flat-bottomed boat and McCabe pushed off from shore. "I keep this here boat for when I need to make an emergency type run over to Hancock to see a guy I know—and when I sure as hell don't wanta see nobody else!" The current caught them, and with McCabe pulling strongly on the oars, they soon reached the Maryland side of the river.

"Are we safe over here?" Allison looked nervous.

"Safer than on the West Virginia side, but no—we ain't safe yet. The Maryland cops are most likely cooperating."

They lifted the suitcases out of the boat and started walking up toward town.

"I know a guy here, done business with him. He'll give us a lift to the airport," McCabe assured her. "Just as long as we stay away from the main roads, we should be O.K."

Yeah, he thought, he'll give us a lift if I part with the last of my cash. That shithead dealer wouldn't help his own mother out for nothing.

* * * *

"That friend of yours gave me the creeps," Allison said as they lugged the baggage up to the airline counter.

"Yeah, he ain't exactly your Boy Scout type, that's for sure!" He'd been ready to punch the guy out long before they got to BWI because of the way he'd been looking at Allison.

"Don't worry," he said. "We'll never see his ugly face again." They picked up their baggage claim checks and boarding passes and went in search of coffee and sandwiches. He slipped his arm around Allison's waist as they strolled through the crowded airport. She looked up at him questioningly. "It's just the brotherly thing to do," he assured her.

McCabe didn't really breathe easy until the big jet was taxiing down the runway. There had always been the chance that the West Virginia cop could have figured out who he was. That dumb sonuvabitch could have decided that he'd kidnapped Allison and taken her over the state line. Maybe they'd even found the Honda by now. Hell, they probably thought he'd done her in—drowned her in the Potomac!

He shot a worried look at Allison. "I'm glad we got away before the cops got started checking airports." She nodded, a relieved look at her eyes. But no sense borrowing trouble, McCabe decided as he sipped whiskey and water and watched the high cloud banks glide by. Well, let 'em stew! He and Allison were on their way! His luck had turned at last!

"McCabe," Allison said, "don't you think that drinking whiskey is a bit un-reverend like?" She gave him a look of mild accusation.

Startled, he set down the drink.

"I guess I should have mentioned this before," she continued, "but, ah, well—I didn't know how you'd take it." She glanced at him uneasily. "At the mission, we, ah, I mean all the missionary staff, have to set an example. You know what I mean—no drinking, no smoking, no, ah, improper language, no immoral life styles. You understand," she said with a somewhat apologetic look in her large dark eyes. "I just thought I should give you some warning since I kind of kidnapped you."

"Understand—warning—kidnapped! That's a laugh!" McCabe sputtered, his 'civilized' act disintegrating. "Do you mean to tell me that this here is my last glass of whiskey? Do you mean to tell me that you waited 'til you got me 30,000 foot up and then laid down the law?" He said indignantly, totally forgetting his own recent resolutions. "Well, I think now that YOU owe ME! What do you think of that?"

Allison smiled. Looking at her, McCabe decided he liked what he saw in her smile. "I guess you're right. I do owe you," she said. "After all, if we're going to be together at the mission, sooner or later we'll have to be man and wife. I accept your proposal, McCabe."

A slow grin, the old McCabe grin, spread over his face. "Proposal—I'm glad you put it that way. I doubt I'd have ever gotten up the nerve to say it half so good. I accept."

Two stewardesses in the rear of the plane watched the young couple locked in a long embrace. "Isn't that the Reverend and his 'sister'?" one asked.

"Sure is," the other replied. "If I could travel with *that* reverend, you could call me his sister, too!" They both laughed.

* * * *

Hours later, as the jet circled over the Bogota Airport, McCabe considered his new situation. He was free, he had Allison, and this place was full of mountains and rivers. What more could a Morgan County boy ask? So he couldn't have a drink. So what? Sure wouldn't have been much booze in Regional Jail neither.

He smiled grimly, then brightened. Of course, there was just the chance that he could cook up a little mash out there in that jungle. Grandpap had turned out some mean white lightening before he'd got religion. Yeah, there was always ways of working things out! Luck was sure as hell turning!

"What do you think of Columbia?" Allison asked as they peered out the plane window.

"Well, actually I been looking at them woods, ah, jungles, and thinking about hunting. First thing I gotta do is git out there and find out what they got that passes for squirrel," McCabe answered thoughtfully. "Then I gotta show you how to fry one up and make some gravy. 'Cause, Honey, we ain't gonna make it in Columbia or nowheres else on that cooking of yours!"

As McCabe stepped off the plane into the blazing sun, he thought his grandpap would be satisfied now—yeah, maybe even proud. His 'hell-fire boy' would be paying his debt to the Lord for years to come, looking after these here savages and dealing with a crazy woman!

Well, he'd sure as hell make the best of it. He already had a few plans.

ROSIE AND MAC

TUESDAY NIGHT, MAY 3rd: Mac McCabe released the handbrake and eased the white Porsche down the drive. The tires crunched lightly over the gravel. He glanced back at the A-frame, but no lights flashed on; no alarms sounded. Soon the cabin sank back into the shadow of the mountain. All was quiet. He guided the sports car down to the main road. As he switched on the headlights, the West Virginia Mountain Rentals sign flashed past. Yeah, people were more relaxed on vacation. They only expected to be ripped off down in the city. Mac revved the engine and headed toward Tanky's place.

The Porsche purred under his touch. In less than 10 minutes, he turned off the Coolfont Road onto Route 9-West. Punching on the radio, Mac grunted with satisfaction as a new country release blasted from the speakers. "The man likes country music. Money didn't make him into no snob," Mac muttered as he pulled out a cigarette. Inhaling the first drag, he started beating on the leather upholstery with the flat of his right hand, keeping time with the twanging guitars.

He smiled. "Well, the owner'll just haveta make a little more money and buy hisself another vehicle. Shitty luck for him, but damn good luck for me."

Not a single hitch, he thought, and he was in for the lion's share. After all his ass was on the line, wasn't it?

Turning off Route 9, Mac headed down Peach tree Hollow Road. Tanky's place was on a side road. You had to be looking for the turn to find it. Tanky was waiting for him. The same country song thumped out loudly in the garage. Mac drove the Porsche through the sagging double doors and jumped out. "Whadaya think, Tanky? Is this here a beauty or what?"

Tanky pushed the greasy cowboy hat back on his head and slowly circled the Porsche. "Ain't bad. Ain't bad at all."

"Should bring a nice piece of change. I had my eye on a new pickup over in Winchester."

"Now boy, don't go getting no big ideas yet. You know the cost of doing business." Tanky propped one hand-tooled boot up carefully on an oil drum. "You ain't nowhere without connections in this business. And connections cost money."

Mac studied the top of Tanky's hat.

"This here's the thing, Mac, You'll do O.K. outta this. Maybe not no new pickup truck. I mean, there's expenses." The two eyed each other in silence. "How about a beer, boy?" Tanky walked toward the door leading to the house. "Naoma, hey Naoma, get us some beer." He moved quickly for a man of his bulk. "What you say, Mac?"

"You done said it all, Tanky." Mac started moving aimlessly around the shop, picking up a tool, examining it, putting it back down. Finally he came face to face with Tanky. A ballpeen hammer dangled loosely from his right hand. "So, Tanky, I was out there risking my ass tonight. If it weren't for me, you wouldn't have no nice, shiny Porsche to ship down to the chop shop in D.C. You wouldn't have nothing. So just how much do you figure my cut might be?"

"Now hold on, Mac, I just can't do no figuring yet. I ain't sure what we can count on down in the city. But look at it thisaway, ain't I always been fair?"

"Fair? I'll show you fair." Mac reached the Porsche in four long strides. Raising the hammer, he brought it down on the left fender. "I'm taking care of your share right now, Tanky. This here is your share!" Mac brought the hammer down repeatedly on the fender.

Running, Tanky reached him and tried vainly to grab the hammer. Mac was not as tall as Tanky, but slim, fast, and wiry. "You sonnavabitch, you give that hammer here. Are you crazy?"

"Yeah, I'm crazy. Crazy for getting into this thing with you."

"Gimme that." Tanky tried to wrestle the hammer away.

"What about my share?" Mac hissed, shoving Tanky against the wall.

"Chrissakes," Naoma shrieked from the door. "What in the hell are you two doing? Oh my God, you done grabbed a wrecked car." Naoma ran toward the men, a bottle of beer swinging in each plump hand. "Stop it, you fools." Her huge breasts strained against the lime green spandex tanktop. The men fell apart, gaping at her.

"Oh, all right, Mac. You made your point. You'll get what you want." Tanky took one of the beers. "You done spilled half of it, woman. What the hell's wrong with you?"

Ignoring Tanky, Naoma handed the other beer to Mac. "What happened to the car?" she demanded, narrowing her eyes at the ballpeen hammer, now in Tanky's hand. She waited. Finally, she turned and stomped off, tight jeans barely containing her ample butt. At the door Naoma turned. "Gene called. He'll be here any minute with the flatbed. There better be something left to load. Ain't nothing more better happen to that car, Tanky, or I'll be back with the ax." She slammed the door.

* * * *

WEDNESDAY, MAY 4th: "Damn Gene," Mac muttered as he tried to maneuver the flatbed through D.C. traffic. He couldn't remember the street name, although he'd been to Vito's place before. Gene would have known. He should have been here. This was a two-man job. Damn Gene. At the last minute he'd run off home—some problem with his woman. Just left, stupid sonnavabitch. Couldn't trust him. Last time Gene would ever be cut in. Finally Mac located the street. He left the flatbed, loaded with the gleaming white Porsche, parked in front of Vito's nondescript garage and banged on the door. Nothing happened.

Not wanting to leave the flatbed unattended, Mac glanced back over his shoulder and silently cursed Gene again. He tried the door; it opened. He walked into total darkness. "What the hell is going on," he muttered, feeling his way along a wall. He remembered that the office was in the back, to the left. Some idiot must have shut things down, forgotten about his delivery.

Growing accustomed to the dark, Mac moved silently toward the back of the building. Oughta cut and run, something not right here, he thought. But what could he do? Get back in the flatbed and drive the Porsche home again? No way. He'd taken enough risks. It was time to unload, get the money and take off. Vito was probably out to lunch, or screwing his secretary. Just because some fool turned the lights off, there was no reason to get spooked. This was payoff time.

Mac reached the office door and eased it open. More darkness. He stood there trying to figure out what to do next. Where was the light switch? He wasn't sure what alerted him first, but suddenly he knew he wasn't alone in the small room. The muscles tensed in the back of his neck. He skirted the room silently. Mac could make out the desk in the center of the room. Was someone slumped over it? Fumbling for his lighter; he flicked it on. Vito was lying over the desk. His throat had been cut. "Oh, sweet Jesus," Mac whispered. "Gotta get outta here."

Suddenly, the garage outside the office door exploded with light and the noise of barked orders, cursing, men running, and equipment being overturned. Somebody was sure as hell searching for something or someone. Mac listened. Was it the cops? Oh shit! He was a sitting duck. No, probably not the cops. These men sounded too angry, too relentless. Vito's "business partners"? They'd probably done Vito in, poor sonnavabitch. They'd sure as hell pop him if they found him here. Mac looked around carefully—no other door, nothing.

He could hear the intruders working their way methodically toward the back of the building. Well, Tanky had had to pick gangsters to do business with, but Tanky wasn't here to face the music.

Then Mac heard another noise, a soft sobbing sound coming from the corner of the room. He edged toward the sound. "Help. Help me, perfavore, aiuto! Get me out of here."

"Where are you?" Mac whispered.

"Here, behind the bookcase."

Looking down, Mac made out the small, huddled figure of a young girl. "Who are you?"

"Rosa. I'm Vito's niece. Who are you?"

"Mac. I'm, eh, sort of a deliveryman. Sure as hell shouldn'ta made this delivery. Look, we gotta get outta here."

"Yes, before they find us. They are bad men."

"How? How can we get out?" Mac could hear the searchers coming closer.

"The window. Help me up. Hurry." The girl crossed herself as she ran past Vito's body.

The small window was set high in the wall. As Mac boosted her up, he realized she wasn't near as young as he'd thought. Pretty filled out for a schoolgirl. She was also agile and quick. In minutes she had the window open. Straddling the frame, she reached down a hand for him.

Breathless and shaken, they found themselves in the narrow alley that ran along the side of the building. Mac grabbed the girl's arm and steered her toward the flatbed truck parked in front. At the corner, they paused. Nothing. By now the men must be in Vito's office. Soon, they'd spot the open window. "Wait here." Mac ran into the street, reached the flatbed, and in minutes had released the Porsche. He didn't have to look around for the girl; they fell into the car at the same time. Mac gunned the engine and the Porsche's tires squealed. They were off.

"Somebody just ran out the front door." The girl was looking back as the Porsche rounded the corner and blended into heavy traffic. "Oh, Grazie Dio." She crossed herself. "We escaped. Now, Where can I go that they can't find me?"

Glancing at her, Mac noted that she was dressed in a short skirt and baggy sweater. The student backpack she wore had given her the schoolgirl appearance. Lots of long, dark curls fell around her shoulders. She was a looker. She was also dangerous as hell. He should put her out at the next corner. Instead, he grinned at her and said, "Say, you ain't American, are you? I like the way you talk. Don't worry, I know a place in the hills where they ain't never gonna find you. Prettiest place in the world in the spring. Ever heard of West Virginia?"

The Porsche crawled through city traffic. When they finally hit the Beltway, Mac relaxed a little. Turning off onto Route I-70 West, he felt free. "We're in the state of Maryland now, have been for a while. After we pass Frederick, You'll get your first look at the mountains."

"We're going to the mountains?"

"Yeah, lots of mountains in West Virginia. We'll get off the Interstate at Hancock, Maryland, cross the Potomac River, and in a few miles hit a little place called Berkeley Springs. I grew up there. Best to avoid the town though. I know a lot of places in the hills and along the Ca'pon River where you'll be safe. Matter of fact, my cousin Jett has a cabin in the hills near the river. Folks living on the back roads are loners, not used to strangers. They're none too friendly to anybody poking around, asking questions."

* * * *

While Mac and the girl drove toward West Virginia, Jett McCabe was trying to tie things up in his Washington, D.C. office. A big man in his mid-thirties, he looked like an older, heavier version of Mac. As a police Sergeant, Jett rated a small desk behind a partition. He wanted to leave for his cabin in West Virginia on Friday, a day earlier than he usually got away. Springtime was the hardest time to sit behind a desk. The redbuds would be in bloom behind the cabin.

Chrissakes, the city was driving him crazy. He only hoped his dumbass cousin, Mac, had left the cabin alone. The last time Mac had crashed there, all his fishing tackle had disappeared. Mac had always had trouble drawing the line between what was his and what belonged to other people. And he wasn't the only McCabe who had this problem. That was one reason Jett had left the West Virginia State Police and moved to the city. He'd gotten tired of arresting his uncles and cousins. "Can't pick your relatives," Jett muttered as he got back to work and opened a new file on the computer. It read: "DeMarco Crime Family."

* * * *

Jimmy DeMarco leafed through the ledger book in Vito's office. Without looking up, he issued orders quietly and concisely. "Mike, check over the flatbed from West Virginia again. Try to find the registration. See if the driver left anything in the cab. Move."

"Joey, get rid of Vito here. You know what to do. I want the word spread that he held out on Jimmy DeMarco." Shutting the ledger, he handed it to his driver. "Rico, we'll take this with us. I want you to check on who Vito did business with in Vest Virginia." DeMarco turned and left the office. The driver followed.

Settled in the Mercedes, DeMarco said, "So, who's the girl who left in the Porsche with the kid from West Virginia?"

"Vito's niece. She showed up a week ago, was in a convent school in Torino."

"Chrissakes, don't tell me I'm going to have to ice a nun?"

"She ain't a nun yet, Boss. That's why Vito brought her over here. He got a letter from the sisters telling him, he's next of kin, see, that she had graduated from high school and was considering taking vows for the convent. He sent for her. Hadn't seen her in fifteen years, since her parents died."

"So, Rico, do you think Vito entrusted this little convent girl with my money? And if she doesn't know anyone in the States, where could she be now?

* * * *

The Porsche labored up the rutted dirt road and stopped. "This is my cousin Jett's place. He's a cop down in the city so nobody's usually here through the week. Whatdaya think"

"It is a good cabin. I like it here on the mountain."

"This here is a really just a hill. But it's a nice, quiet spot. Let's go in and see if we can find something to eat. I'm starved." Mac rented a small apartment in Berkeley Springs, but it hadn't seemed like a good idea to go back there tonight.

"So, your cousin's a policeman." The girl smiled. "We have families, also, like this in Italy. They may not agree on anything, but they all go to Mass on Sunday and then sit down for dinner together. After all, family is family, yes?" Her smile made her really beautiful.

"Yeah, well Jett McCabe ain't that forgiving. Don't have an understanding bone in his body." Mac realized that Jett would be mad as hell right now if he knew that Mac and the Italian girl were sitting in front of his fireplace. As far as Jett was concerned, his cousin Mac was a two-bit crook and hustler, and he would peg the girl as Mafia family. Mac grinned as he pictured Jett's reaction to the hot Porsche parked outside. Well, too bad. Smartass sonnavabitch would be in for a surprise.

"Will I meet this Cousin Jett? I would like to thank him for his hospitality."

"I don't think so, eh…I don't remember your name?"

"Rosa, Rosa Maria Teresa Delucca."

"Yeah," Mac said, "but I can't call you that. How about Rosie?"

"Rosie is O.K. Yes, I like it. It's American."

"It's American. I been wondering how you learned to speak English so good, Rosie?"

"English? Well, at the school we had English classes. I also talk French, better French than English, I think. I lived near the French border and many of the nuns who taught us were French. Do you really think I talk good English?" She grinned.

Probably better than mine. Another thing that puzzles me, what were you doing in Vito's office today? What happened?"

Rosie's face crumpled. She put a hand over her mouth, but couldn't stop tears. Gingerly, Mac moved closer and put a comforting arm around her.

"I had gone to help him count everything. You say 'inventory.' It was a small thing I could do to help. Zio Vito, Uncle Vito, had been so kind to me. We were working in the storeroom when he looked out the window and got very upset. A car had driven up in the alley, you see. His face went very white, and he told me to run and hide in the restroom. 'Sta attenta! Corri!' he told me. I did what he said. I could hear angry voices. My uncle kept saying, 'Jimmy, per favore.' I heard him scream, 'Aiuto, Dio mio, Aiuto!' He was calling for help, pleading for his life. He kept repeating, 'Casa mia, casa mia.' Rosie shuddered. "Then all was quiet. I heard the men leaving. Finally I snuck back to Uncle Vito's office. I found him—E morto, dead. I should have left then, but I was too terrified. I know now that he threw the Mafia off, sending them to his home to search for…for what they wanted, so that I could escape. But I was idiota! I just hid there, crying. And then you came. You looked too young to be a Mafioso, but you had that beard, so I wasn't sure at first." She looked up at him. "You and I, we could both be dead along with Uncle Vito."

"Yeah, I guess we could." Mac stroked his short, closely trimmed beard. "So a beard makes you a gangster? Maybe I oughta shave it off."

"No, no, I like it. It's just that I was very scared and nervous then."

Poor kid, he thought, she's sure as hell been through a lot. "Don't worry, nobody ain't gonna mess with you no more, Rosie. You got my word on it."

Later they finished a dinner of canned beans and sardines, and Rosie seemed a little more relaxed. "So what you planning to do now, Rosie? Go back to Italy? You got people there?" Mac stretched out his long legs and pulled out a smoke. The warmth of the fire made the small cabin cozy. He smiled at Rosie, hoping her answer would be no.

"Oh, no, not Italy. I have no family there anymore. Vito was my only family, and I couldn't even see him properly buried." Rosie looked down. "He was good to me. If it weren't for Uncle Vito I probably would be a novice by now."

"A novice?"

"I'm sorry. I forgot you are not Catholic. Everybody at home is. A novice is, well, a kind of apprentice nun, a junior nun."

"A nun! You wanted to become a nun? Oh, no, I can't believe it." Mac stood up and confronted her. "Get up!"

Rosie stood up. Her dark eyes never left his narrowed blue eyes. Very slowly, Mac lowered his lips to hers. His kiss was light, but lingering.

Rosie pulled away first. She was laughing. "No, Mac, I never really thought I'd have made a good nun. But, you see, I'd been in an Ursuline Convent School ever since my parents died when I was very young. I knew no other life. So when I graduated, it seemed like a good idea. I had no future."

"Well, you do now, Rosie. You do now."

"I don't know what the future will bring, but I know it's here, on this side of the ocean. There is something I must do now, Mac. Come and sit down. I need to talk to you."

"What you need to do," Mac said as he sat next to her, "is to put as much space between you and those gangsters as we can get."

"Yes, but first I must find the Sisters of the Ursuline Convent here in America. I have a regalo, a gift for them from Uncle Vito. They will pray for his soul."

Mac stared at her. She was sure one complicated woman. "Gift? Vito? I don't understand."

"Well, it's simple. Until I deliver this, eh, gift, neither Uncle Vito or I will be free. I must do it, but how? Will you help me, Mac?"

Her smile almost made him consider this crazy scheme. But he said, "I wouldn't even know where to start." Rosie really should have picked somebody better qualified to help save Uncle Vito's soul.

* * * *

THURSDAY, MAY 5th: In the morning, Mac headed for Tanky's place. Rosie was still sleeping in the cabin's only bedroom. Mac had bunked on the couch. Chrissakes, he'd never had any trouble with women, but what could he do with a little nun? The best thing to do was keep his distance.

About an half mile from Tanky's, Mac pulled off the road and was able to maneuver the Porsche up an abandoned logging road. "Can't never be too careful," he muttered as he wiped the car clean. Continuing on foot, he approached the garage from the rear. He stood at the edge of the woods and waited. His old truck was still parked by the garage. Checking out the ramshackle house next to the garage, he noticed that Naomi's station wagon was gone. Everything was quiet. After about ten minutes, Mac walked slowly along the side of the building and slipped inside. The door had been ajar. Silence. No country music blared from the radio, no movement, nobody home.

Mac spotted Tanky over in the grease pit. At first, he thought Tanky was just standing there, resting against the side of the pit. When he reached him, he saw that Tanky's head was twisted at an unnatural angle. His throat had been slit, just like Vito's. Someone had propped him up in the grease pit. Poor bastard, Mac thought. Looks like they worked him over pretty good before they killed him. He'd have handed me to them on a platter if he could've, but he sure as hell didn't deserve nothing like this. Looking around, Mac saw that there weren't even signs of a struggle. He figured that Tanky had been taken by surprise, as he was a big man and would have gone down swinging. "Damn them all to hell," Mac muttered.

Mac found Tanky's handgun in the bottom drawer of the old desk and shoved it into his belt. He was gathering up two boxes of hollow point bullets, when he spotted a West Virginia license plate in the back of the drawer. He slipped it inside his jacket. Stuffing the bills from the cash box into his pockets, he headed toward the door.

Outside, Mac pressed against the side of the building. He edged closer to the truck, alert for any unusual sounds or movements. It was a beautiful, clear spring morning, and birds were making a racket in the nearby trees. Relaxing a little, Mac told himself that even these crazy hoods wouldn't hang around. Easing the keys from his pocket, he ran for the truck. Too late, he realized that his tires had been slashed while he'd been inside. The air was slowly seeping out of all four tires.

The first shot landed about five feet ahead of him. Hitting the ground, Mac snaked along on this belly until he had the truck between himself and his attackers. Bullets hit the ground all around him. They weren't trying to kill him, or he'd be dead by now. He realized that they needed him alive so he could lead them to Rosie. Bastards!

Rolling into the cover of the woods, he was up and running instantly. Zigzagging around trees, he dove into the cover of some overhanging evergreen branches. New spring brambles fused the thicket into a thick screen. Behind him, his pursuers were bulldozing their way through the woods. He fingered the gun at his waist.

The thrashing noises faded. Mac started off silently, heading deeper into the woods. Here he was in control. He had hunted every inch of this mountainside; it was his turf. They could kiss his butt. Moving fast and shortcutting over rough terrain, it still took him over two hours to reach Jett's cabin.

Rosie was nowhere to be found. Panicking, he wondered if the Mob had found her here. But, no, impossible. There were no fresh tire tracks, and that bunch were no woodsmen. "Rosie," he shouted, throwing out all caution. "Rosie, where are you?"

Rosie emerged from the woods, carrying an armful of redbud blossoms. She was smiling. Mac stopped and stared at her. "Thank God you're safe." He didn't want to alarm her, but he had to get her away.

"These are my 'regalo,' my gift to Uncle Vito." She laid the flowers under a huge oak tree, then crossed herself.

Back inside the cabin Mac said, "There's been a problem with the truck. I'll tell you about it later. Right now, we gotta get outta here and quick." They gathered up the rest of Jett's canned food, a couple of flashlights, and two sleeping bags from the bedroom. Rosie was calm; she didn't ask any questions. Mac fashioned two packs out of the sleeping bags and they started off through the woods. He had the satisfaction of picturing the look on Jett's face when he finally showed up at the cabin. He'd be some kinda pissed. He did feel a stab of guilt when they passed the spot where he'd taken his first buck at the age of 12. Jett had been with him, his teacher, his friend. Well, Jett had changed; he was a cop now.

It was tough going for the first 10 or 15 minutes. When they finally reached a stretch of level ground, they stopped to catch their breaths. Rosie looked so scared that Mac was concerned. "We'll have to rough it for a while, Rosie. But don't worry, we'll make it to your convent. That's what you want, isn't it?"

A look of astonishment flashed over Rosie's face. She struggled out of her pack, threw her arms around Mac, and kissed him. "You are wonderful, Mac, wonderful. Grazie!" The rest of her words came out in rapid-fire Italian. She grabbed his hand. "We can do it, Mac. You are a good man!"

The sun was directly overhead when Rosie and Mac reached the Cacapon River. They had followed an old game trail, which made the going easy. Mac had had time to think. Actually, he felt great. Maybe if he helped Rosie with this crazy scheme, just maybe, she'd think he was a decent guy. But he had no idea how they were going to pull it off. They had no vehicle, little money, and no idea of their destination. Plus, the Mob was on their tail. Mac looked around at the rugged sandstone cliffs and the rushing spring flood river, and he knew no one would ever find them here. They were safe for now.

By evening, Mac had thrown together a lean-to of pine branches and had gotten a fire going. Rosie had helped gather branches and driftwood. When they had finished and were heating cans of macaroni for dinner, Mac filled her in on what had happened to Tanky.

"Dio mio, that poor man. I will pray for him along with Uncle Vito." Rosie looked like she was ready to burst into tears. "I'm so scared, Mac. We can't let them find us." She sat, staring into the fire.

"I been thinking, Rosie, we should really get outta the country—Canada, Mexico. I ain't got no goodbyes to say here. Whadaya think?"

"Yes. I know the Mafia better than you do, and I say yes. As long as we can get to an Ursuline Convent. That I have to do." Her small mouth set in a determined line.

"Yeah, the convent. That there is a problem."

* * * *

On Thursday evening the two State Troopers had been at the Minns' home for at least two hours. The younger officer gestured toward a chair, "Mrs. Minns, you gotta sit down." He stood by helplessly as Naoma shrieked and wailed. All he wanted to do was complete her statement and get the hell out of there. The team that had dealt with the stiff in the garage had had it easy.

"Don't tell me whata do. Where was you when poor Tanky was killed? Murdered in cold blood. Where was the cops then?" Naoma lunged at the officer and started shaking him. "You're about as worthless as they get. What are you good for?"

It took both the trooper and his partner to detach Naoma and lead her to a chair. One of them brought her a coke. "When did you return home, Mrs. Minns?"

"I done told you fools once. On Thursday mornings I always take Mother Minns for her treatment down to Martinsburg. The kids all go along to K-Mart. We never get home till evening. That's when I found poor Tanky." She shrieked again and started to sob.

"Did Mr. Minns have any known enemies?" The second trooper spoke loudly.

"Known enemies!" Try that there sonnavabitch Mac McCabe. He done threatened Tanky with a ballpeen hammer just Tuesday night. You look into what Mac was up to this morning."

The troopers looked at each other. "Do you have any idea how much cash Mr. Minns kept here?"

"Cash," Naoma screamed. "Hell, how should I know? But anything you find is mine, hear."

"Could you tell us who your husband's business contacts were?"

"Husband! Tanky ain't never been my husband. That was Elmer Minns, rest his soul, who built up this here garage." Naoma blew her nose loudly. "No, Tanky was only my brother-in-law."

"Yes Ma'am, but you being close to him and all, you must have known who he did business with."

"I don't know nothing, nothing. I need a drink and a cigarette. Just you look for that bastard, Mac McCabe, I tell you. He's a maniac." She turned and left the room.

The troopers watched her stomp away, then turned back to their notes. "Sure looks like a professional job, but that don't seem possible up here in Morgan County," the younger trooper looked puzzled. "And which one of them damn Mc-Cabes is this Mac?"

"Not sure, but we better call in Sgt. Kincaid. Nate grew up around here. He knows all these twisted family relationships. Besides, he has contacts down in Washington, D.C."

* * * *

Nate Kincaid's contact down in D.C., Jett McCabe, sat in his office in front of the computer screen. By now, he'd fleshed out many of the twisted family relationships of the DeMarco crime family. He was going over the homicide report on DeMarco's latest hit, a small time auto parts butcher named Vito Delucca. Taking a break, he lit a cigarette. Tomorrow, he thought, he'd be up in West Virginia and away from this mess.

* * * *

FRIDAY, MAY 6th: The next morning dawned cold and damp at the campsite along the river. Mac knew there would be rain before noon. Time to pull out. He had another spot in mind. After an hour of dragging their gear through rough country, Rosie and Mac reached several deserted summer cottages in a spot where the river formed a deep pool behind the old power dam. "This here is Briary Bottom," Mac gestured toward the cottages. "These folks have young kids, so they never show up through the week until summer." He pointed to the old, rambling cottage closest to the woods.

The cottage was shut down for the season, so Mac had to tinker with the plumbing. He was looking around for tools when he heard Rosie yell from the kitchen. "Mac, Mac, I've found everything here to make spaghetti sauce. I'll make you a real Italian dish. Look, red wine. I even found wineglasses. Bene, bene!"

Later, as they ate dinner, Mac noticed that Rosie had decorated with some white emergency candles and a large water glass of wild flowers. When this was over, he'd buy her a room full of flowers. Mac fingered the stem of his wineglass. This was all great, but right now he'd sure as hell rather have a cold beer with steak and home fries. But he said, "Best damn spaghetti I ever ate. Love it."

Rosie grinned. "What kind of food did you eat at home, Mac, when you were a kid?"

"When Mom was still alive, we ate good. Lots of game, fish, stuff from the garden. That woman was a worker." He shifted uncomfortably. "She was on second shift over at the sewing factory, but she still took time to make life good. After she died, things was different."

"Different?"

"Yeah, well me and Dad managed best we could. I started cooking about that time. Ever had chicken fried squirrel and gravy?"

"You're kidding." Rosie grimaced.

"Not a whit. Gotta eat what's around. 'Why go to the store?' my ol' man always said. 'Just you run down to the river, boy, and get us some fish.'"

"Where is your papa now?"

"Dead too, most likely. Fact is, I don't know. Been on my own since I was 17. Stayed off and on with Jett. But then his kid died in an accident and his woman left him, so he started to drink. He wasn't all that bad to be around then, but when he finally got sober again he turned into a real tightass. Moved down to the city. He shoulda stayed here where he belonged. That's his problem, not the booze." He lifted his wineglass. "Nothing wrong with a little drink. To the chef, to Rosie." He smiled at her. Glancing out the window, he saw a light rain falling. But here in the candlelight, it was fine. He relaxed and pulled out a smoke.

* * * *

"Well, if this just don't beat all." Jett McCabe bellowed as he surveyed his cabin on Friday evening. "Toted off my food, stole my sleeping bags, and my flashlights." He stomped around the small rooms. "All I'm left with is a wilted bunch of redbud blossoms. Takes a damn nerve!" He flung the flowers out the window. "I bet I have that sonnuvabitch Mac to thank for this," he muttered. "Try to do the kid a favor and this is how he pays me back."

It took Jett a while to spot the three one hundred dollar bills laying on the table near the empty vase. "Well, will you look at this. Sure lets out my cousin, Mac. Cheap bastard never had no three hundred dollars, and flowers just ain't his style." He was still fingering the bills when the phone rang. Picking it up, he wondered who the hell even knew he was here on a Friday.

"Jett, this is Nate Kincaid. You got a minute?"

Jett groaned. Nate Kincaid was a plodding, methodical bastard who'd always rubbed him the wrong way. They had been rookies together years ago.

"This here's the thing, Jett. We got a problem murder case. You remember Tanky Minns? Could you meet me at Tanky's place at 7:30 tomorrow morning? I could really use your help."

"Tanky Minns? Yeah, I remember him. Dead, eh. O.K., I'll be there, Nate." Jett groaned again and hung up.

* * * *

SATURDAY, MAY 7th: About 3:00 A.M. Mac awoke suddenly. The glare of headlights flashed through the window into the room. A car drove slowly by and stopped. Alert now, he rolled off the couch and, crouching, moved to the window. "What the hell," he mumbled. A station wagon loaded with teenagers had pulled in next door. Six-packs of beer were being unloaded amid loud laughter and shouting. A fat kid was tugging at the canoe on the car-top carrier. "Holy shit! They're here to party." Mac turned to find Rosie at his side.

"What's going on?"

"Damn kids. They're just out raising hell, partying all night. Oughta be home in bed." He put an arm around Rosie, who was shivering. "Look, we gotta get outta here. Them crazy kids could take it into their heads to crash in here. They're all about half loaded." Ironic, he thought. A couple of years ago he'd have been out there with them.

In a half an hour Rosie and Mac had gathered their belongings and slipped out the side door into the woods. The rain had turned to mist and a full moon was trying to break through the clouds. Going was a little rough until they cleared the cottage area; then they used the flashlights.

"I know a real isolated place not far away," Mac grinned encouragingly at Rosie. "Should have remembered it before. I done some carpentry work for the owner last year. He'll still be in Florida now. It's perfect."

Rosie and Mac reached the house set high above the Cacapon River just as the sun was rising. The river was framed on this side by imposing sandstone cliffs. From the deck they gazed down at white, swirling water, overhung by the new green of willows. "This is so beautiful. It's like a scene from a painting," Rosie said.

"It should be safe here," Mac glanced at the towering cliffs and the twisting river below. God, I hope so, he thought. He knew they had to try to get clean away, and soon.

They walked around the large deck and found a covered hot tub in one corner. "What is this thing?" Rosie asked.

"That there is a hot tub. You fill in with hot water and soak. Relaxes the hell outta you. I used to sneak into the hot tub at the resort. They fired me for all kinds of things, but they never even knew about that."

"A hot tub," Rosie said. "I would like to try that one day."

* * * *

Exhausted, they slept most of the morning. Alone in the master bedroom, Rosie found it hard to sleep in the soft king sized bed. When she finally dozed off, her dreams took her back to the deck over the wild river.

Standing by the hot tub, she dropped her towel and climbed into the steaming water. She sat on a narrow ledge and leaned her head back. The water washed over her and eased the tension away.

Wrapped in a towel, Mac appeared and knelt down next to the tub. He lifted her hair from the water and wrapped the long strands gently around his hand. He started to kiss her neck, then reached down to kiss her lips. All the while, he murmured words of love.

Rosie stretched out her hand. "Here, come into the water beside me."

Mac threw his towel onto the deck and slid into the water. He pulled her to him and kissed her with great tenderness.

* * * *

Mac tossed and turned in one of the lower bunk beds down the hall. About eleven o'clock he got up and started hunting around the place for fishing gear. He knew he'd seen rods and lures here last year. He gathered together a usable assortment and headed down a steep, overgrown path to the river. Standing on a large flat rock, he cast into the clear water and began to relax. As the sun beat down, he stretched his body out over the warm stone. Soon his eyes were shut and the fishing rod dangled from his hand. Mac's dreams took him to the steaming hot tub.

Lounging in the water, he looked up and saw Rosie, clad in the briefest bikini. She slid into the opposite side of the tub and smiled at him, beckoning. When he eagerly splashed over, she held up her hand, palm out. He stopped. She offered her hand to be kissed. Reaching past her hand, he kissed her on the lips. At first she responded, then pulled away and started to cry.

"Oh, no, not before the marriage. The nuns told me of men like you."

"Marriage," Mac gasped. "Look, Rosie, we been traveling together for four days now. Even the nuns would have to take that into account. Here in West Virginia we'd almost be common law man and wife by now." He lunged toward her, but she disappeared beneath the water.

Mac awoke to find a large fish tugging on his line.

* * * *

They cooked the trout over a charcoal grill on the deck. Rosie looked at him shyly and seemed to recoil when he asked her to set the grill utensils on the cover of the nearby hot tub.

"I'll find another place," she murmured. Mac wondered what she had to be shy about. He was the one with the lustful dreams.

The warm May afternoon foretold rain, and the scent of lilacs hung heavy in the air. Rosie had found the delicate purple flowers growing near the back door and pinned one in her hair. She did things like this, Mac mused. The girls he usually ran around with would have thought this was corny. Right now, he couldn't even remember any of their names. He was watching Rosie. She had found a couple of wooden deck chairs and was dragging them over to the railing. He watched the way her body moved in the tight jeans. They had found some boy's clothes in one of the bedrooms. At first, she hadn't wanted to take anything, even though her short skirt was hardly good for hiking. But finally she had agreed. Well, the jeans made her look different—American. It was all he could do to keep his hands off her.

Looking down over the railing at the racing water below, Rosie said, "The river looks dangerous."

"No, not really dangerous. It's a rough ride though. Run these rapids many a time." Mac gestured downward. "My ol' man had a beaten up John boat. Leaked like hell." He grinned at her. "You know, that's the way life oughta be, just one hellava river trip…not this 9 to 5 shit. I just ain't cut out for that kinda life."

She sat down. "So, Mac, in West Virginia life is just one long river trip?"

"No, I guess I gave you the wrong idea, but it should be. It sure as hell should be. What do you want outta life anyway, Rosie?"

"Now? Now I just want to live. But later…yes, in Canada, I want to have children, and a nice home for them. I like kids, you see. I learned to look after small ones at the convent school." Her large, dark eyes were smiling up at him.

Kids? Well, Mac guessed this was a good sign. But it didn't sound like the free, wild ride through life he had in mind.

"So, Mac, what kind of job do you want in Canada?"

Job? Kids? He shifted uncomfortably against the deck railing. But this was what he wanted, wasn't it? "I can do whatever I need to do to get by, carpentry, mechanic work, drive a truck…whatever," he told Rosie, and lit his last cigarette. It started to rain again.

* * * *

When Jett got down to Minns' garage on Saturday morning, he hadn't decided whether to mention his own robbery to Nate yet. He was surprised to see Mac's old truck sitting on its rims in the parking lot. What in hell could Mac have been doing here? What had happened to the truck? And where was the kid?

Nate was waiting for him. "What you got?" Jett asked.

"Got a Mob style hit. That's why I called you in. I know it don't seem likely here in the hills, but it sure as hell looks like it."

Jett listened with growing apprehension, thinking of the increasing Mafia activity in his D.C. precinct. But it would be tough for the Mob to operate up here. This wasn't their home ground.

Nate finally completed his long, blow-by-blow account, from the missing cash box money and the disappearance of Tanky's handgun to the discovery of the hot Porsche. "Damn if the Porsche hadn't been heisted up here, from some tourist. Found it in the woods, not a mile from here. Strange thing was somebody had beat in one fender. Crazy? eh? And there's no sense talking to Mrs. Minns. She's a lunatic."

"Yeah, always was. Well, I'll see what I can get together down in D.C. that could be helpful. I'll FAX it up to you, Nate."

Both men were silent for a while. "Eh, one more thing, Jett. This Mrs. Minns keeps accusing your cousin, Mac. And his truck is sitting out there in the lot, all four tires slashed. The investigating officers decided the killers thought it was Tanky's truck and were making another statement. But I don't buy that dumbass idea. Now I know he ain't much account, but I can't believe Mac's involved in this mess."

"Mac's an asshole. But he ain't dumb enough to get mixed up with the Mafia. When I get aholda him, I'll find out what's up." Jett reached for his keys. He'd had enough of Nate Kincaid. "I'm gonna find out what Mac's truck is doing here. You got any other suspects?"

"We don't have no suspects right now. Tanky Minns was too smooth to go around making enemies close to home. I don't know, though, Morgan County ain't like it used to be. Time was when you knew all the crooks. Hell, probably related to half of them." Nate followed Jett toward the garage door. "Now, you just don't know. Bunch of new people moving up here from the city. Most of them are crazier than hoots. Just yesterday, a guy went up to his summer place in Briary Bottom. Called in and said the cottage had been broken into, but he claims some damn fool left a water glass full of flowers and a one hundred dollar bill. No local job, I'll guarantee that."

Jett stopped walking and turned around. "What did you just say?" he asked Kincaid.

* * * *

Back at the cabin, Jett tried phoning Mac, then finally called his landlady. She hadn't seen Mac for days, but she mentioned acidly that he owed her two months back rent and hoped Jett would be good for it. "Damn boy is worthless. Tried to get him a good job in the city. Tried to get him to join the Army, but no, he don't want no normal life," Jett muttered as he climbed back into the Bronco and headed over to Tanky's place again.

As he approached the house, country music blasted through the open front door. A baby wailed somewhere inside. Jett hesitated, recalling his previous encounters with Naoma back in the days when he'd been with the West Virginia State Police. Why had he come? He probably wouldn't get anything sensible out of her anyway. Just then the screen door banged open. A large woman, twice the size of Naoma, filled the doorway. Tiny black eyes peered out under a high pile of orange curls. Wobbling double chins and flushed, puffy cheeks encased cupid bow lips. A huge, flowered, tent-like covering hid the rest of her body. She wasn't smiling.

"Is Naoma in?" Jett asked, half-hoping she'd be out. "I'm Jett McCabe. She knows me."

"Naoma don't wanna see nobody, especially no cops."

"And I sure ain't gonna talk to no McCabes," Naoma yelled from inside the house. "Tell that asshole to clear out, Mother Minns."

"You done heard her, get out," Mother Minns tried to push the door closed.

Jett shoved his foot in the doorway. "Listen up, I'm trying to locate the owner of some recovered money. Need to know what was missing from the garage." Jett shifted his weight, not budging from the doorway. "I'm so sorry, Ma'am, about the death of your son. I knew him well." He grinned.

The mountain in the doorway hesitated. "You knew my Tanky?" She started to bawl loudly. "Naoma, this here guy knew Tanky."

"Of course he knew Tanky," Naoma yelled back. "Sonnuvabitch arrested him enough times." But Jett saw her walking toward the door. She was wearing a bright pink spandex top, tight black jeans, and four-inch silver high heels. Hands on bulging hips, she said, "What the hell you want, Jett? Ain't you able to see we're in mourning here."

She's sure looking older, Jett thought. Now it took twice as much makeup and half as much spandex to produce the same product as a few years ago. The last time he'd seen her, she'd been a blonde. Now her hair was a brassy orange, a couple of shades brighter than old Ma Minns'.

"Naoma, I just come by to try to do you a favor."

"Ha! What favor?"

He ducked in through the doorway. The room was cluttered, but clean. A TV blared in the corner. Twanging country music blasted from somewhere in the rear of the house. The baby still wailed. Tanky's picture, surrounded by withered flower arrangements, adorned the mantel. Jett could see that Tanky was already on his way to sainthood with the Minns clan.

"Well, eh, this here's the thing. Certain amounts of money have been recovered, and I'm trying to trace the rightful owner. If you could just answer a few questions, it really would be a help. Let's start with Tanky and Mac. What kinda business deal did they have going?"

"Business deal? What the hell you talking about? I don't know nothing about no deals."

"Why was Mac here on Tuesday night then?"

"How should I know," Naoma started to move around the room, stopping in front of Tanky's picture. "Tanky was good to everybody, even Mac. Give him a beer that night. That was just like him." She blew her nose loudly. Mother Minns started bawling again.

"Was Tanky dealing with anybody down in the city? Could he have had any enemies there? Have you seen any strangers hanging around here?"

"Enemies! Strangers! You just look to Mac McCabe for an enemy. He done attacked poor Tanky with a ballpeen hammer. I told them other dumb cops all this, and ain't nothing been done." Naoma began wailing.

"Shit," Jett muttered. "Listen, Naoma, I know this is hard for you. But the police report stated that the only cash missing in the garage was roughly fifty dollars from the cash box. Much more than this has been recovered, so I figure there had been some business deal in the works. Maybe something had gotten screwed up, gone sour?"

The mention of money had an instantly calming effect. "More money," Naoma blubbered. "Well, maybe Gene Gray would know. He done some work for Tanky from time to time. Guess I forgot to mention Gene to the State Boys. Yeah, Gene stopped by on Tuesday evening."

Jett was already edging toward the door. He'd gotten what he wanted. "O.K. Well, here's my card if you think of anything else. Thanks."

"Not so fast," Naoma was right behind him. "When will I get my money? Left here with no man, me and my kids and grandkids, and poor Mother Minns here."

"Let you know soon," Jett shouted over his shoulder as he bolted for the Bronco. Throwing the truck into gear, he floored the accelerator and headed for Great Cacapon, a small town about six miles west of Berkeley Springs. It was time to see old Gene. He never had liked the sneaky little bastard, so this ought to be a pleasure, Jett thought as he lit a cigarette.

* * * *

Gene was skinning a large catfish near the Cacapon River, which ran behind his trailer. His short, pudgy fingers worked skillfully. Concentrating on his task, he didn't hear Jett slip up behind him. "Morning, Gene."

"Oh my God Almighty." Gene jumped, dropped the big catfish, and brandished the skinning knife. "Damn you, Mc-Cabe. Sneaking up on a person like that. What the hell you want?"

They eyed each other in the lengthening silence. Gene finally bent down and retrieved the fish. Jett noticed that his hand shook. Gene's light blue eyes were watering. His breathing was shallow and rapid. Deciding to try a long shot, Jett moved closer and smiled. "Gene, what can you tell me about Tanky Minns, Mac, and the Mafia?"

Gene's labored breathing seemed to stop; the fish again slipped out of his grasp. "Nothing. I don't know nothing."

"Naoma Minns says you do. All I want is the name of your D.C. contact. Fact is, you and Naoma could both be in danger. I work in D.C. I know what these guys are like." Hell, if they look for Mac long enough, Jett thought grimly, he, himself, could even be in danger.

Gene's doughy complexion became paler. "Vito Delucca," he whispered. "He runs a small specialty garage in D.C."

Jett nodded. Things were falling into place. "What about Mac? When's the last time you seen Mac? Anybody been asking around for him?"

Gene looked down and mumbled,"I ain't seen him since last Tuesday night. But I heard he's around. Honest, you're the first one asking."

"Yeah, well you just tell Georgia you'll be gone for a few hours." Jett said as he slipped the cuffs on Gene. "You need to talk to Nate Kincaid."

* * * *

At 2:00 P.M. Jett was back at his desk in D.C. First, he requested a search on the serial numbers from the four recovered one hundred dollar bills. Then, he spent the afternoon going over data on the DeMarco family. The computer screen displayed names, birth dates, last known addresses, criminal records, etc. Jett knew many of these hoods, including

DeMarco, by sight. Under "known associates," Vito's name popped up. The program had already been updated to include his date of death.

Jett picked up the phone and called for the homicide file on Vito Delucca. By the end of the day, he had digested most of the available information on Vito's murder. One fact stood out, a flatbed truck with a West Virginia plate had been parked in front of Vito's garage on Wednesday, the day of Vito's death. Efforts to trace the registration had been unsuccessful, but two clear sets of prints had been lifted. No matches so far.

Drinking a third cup of coffee, Jett speculated on what he had. Vito and Tanky had some kind of deal going. He wrote No. 1—Deal at the top of a note pad and thought of the hot Porsche found hidden near Tanky's garage. He also thought of the Porsche's dented fender and Naomi's story of Mac and the ballpeen hammer. Mac was probably the runner, and one of those sets of prints was his. He added No. 2—Mac. Vito's Italian niece, Rosa, turned up missing on the same day her uncle was murdered. He wrote No. 3—Rosa.

Homicide had labeled Vito's murder a gangland execution. And the motive? Well, it seemed Vito had been holding out on Jimmy DeMarco. Jett wrote No. 4—DeMarco. He bet the serial numbers on the recovered money from West Virginia would match a list of serialized bills from a recent heist involving DeMarco. He completed the list with No. 5—Money.

So it was pretty clear. Mac and the girl had the money up in West Virginia, and the Mob was hot on their heels. Putting it all together, Jett realized that Mac was a damn stupid kid who didn't know what he was into.

Jett left a call on Nate Kincaid's office recorder. He wanted to know what, if anything, had been learned from Gene. He figured it was time to head back to West Virginia and look after his dumbass cousin.

In the Bronco, fortified with another cup of coffee, Jett tried to calculate where Mac and the girl could be. So far, he calculated, they'd stuck to places that Mac was familiar with.

After all, he would naturally hide in the mountains where he'd grown up. He knew Morgan County, and this would probably work for him and the girl if they stayed put. But that fool, Mac, had never stayed put anywhere. And when they surfaced, they'd be in danger. Jett's mind raced over the possibilities. They'd need supplies, food, gas, etc. Did they really have the mobster's money? This seemed unlikely. If Mac had cash, he'd be long gone. But if Mac needed money, Jett knew how he'd probably get it, and this thought scared him the most. What would flush them out? Who would they contact? What about the girl? Damn Mac and his women. Damn fool! Nothing was worth having the Mafia on your tail.

When Jett pulled off the Interstate at Hancock, Maryland, it had started to rain. He stopped at the Park 'n Dine for a sandwich and home fries. He would have much rather thrown down a couple of cold beers at the bar across the street, but he couldn't do booze anymore. This thought triggered the uncomfortable memory of a younger Mac. Mac had helped him out several times when he had been trying to beat a serious drinking problem. With a grimace, Jett remembered one particular summer night at the cabin. Mac had sat up all night with him, helping him fend off the demons, pouring out hidden supplies of Jim Beam. Jett conceded that he owed the kid. He at least owed him enough to try to keep Mac alive. Damn stupid kid wasn't making it easy.

Jett wolfed down the sandwich, remembering that he hadn't eaten all day. He ordered another sandwich and a piece of pie. Looking around at the few late evening regulars and handful of travelers, he tried to work out the puzzle. Where do people go when they're under stress, scared, and in need of reassurance? Where would these people go? He checked out an elderly couple in a corner booth. The frail, white-haired woman wore a large silver cross, which glinted in the glare of the florescent lights. "Bingo," he said quietly.

That heathen, Mac, was out of this picture. But what about the girl? He tried to recall the paragraph from Vito's homicide report: "Rosa Delucca, 18 years old, Italian citizen, orphan, raised in a convent school, planning to become a nun." He added what he knew about Rosa— *Left payment for anything she took.* Well, the girl had a conscience, he thought. And he knew where she'd go. The Catholic Church in Berkeley Springs would be an easy stake-out.

Before he left the restaurant, he dialed Kincaid's home phone number from the pay phone. Nate answered on the second ring.

"Nate, this is Jett. Anything new?"

"Glad you called, Jett. Thanks for the FAX on the De-Marco family. Listen, I didn't get too much outta that screw-ball, Gene. He knows a lot more then he's saying. He's pretty scared. I can tell you that."

"If you get any stolen vehicle reports, call me Nate, no matter how late it is. I have a feeling something's gonna break." On the ride over to the cabin Jett mentally added the last item to his list, No. 6—Gene.

* * * *

Mac left the cliff top house about 9:00 P.M. on Saturday. They'd set up an escape plan in case anyone showed up, and he'd cautioned Rosie to keep the curtains drawn. Now he wasn't taking any chances. The steady rain made the night cold and foggy, but Mac made good time. He figured the low water bridge would be flooded out, so he crossed the river downstream. He left the old boat he had "borrowed" tied to a tree. The owner would find it if he started searching soon.

Looking back at the river, Mac realized how lucky he'd been to make it across. The brown, rushing water was spilling over the banks. If he hadn't known to cross at the bend, where the current ran near the shore, he'd never have made it. Hell, he'd be on his way to the Potomac! The problem was that he had to get to Great Cacapon, get his business over with Gene, grab a vehicle, and get back for Rosie very quickly. Gusting wind was driving the rain in cold sheets. He decided he had better pick up a 4-wheel drive. He'd probably have to take the back road over the mountain, and it was sure to be washed out and treacherous tonight. Damn Gene! Mac knew the sneaky bastard probably wouldn't be much help anyway.

* * * *

Gene fiddled nervously with the TV antenna, twirling the pole back and forth in his short, stubby fingers. He was already drenched. After each new location, he'd yell in through the trailer window, "Georgia, can't you see nothing yet?"

The wind had picked up, so Gene braced his feet and rotated the antenna again. When he looked up, he was face to face with Mac. The look in Mac's eyes unnerved him. "What the hell you want, McCabe? I'm tired of you bastards sneaking up on me."

"Why, Gene, you don't sound too glad to see me. Couldn't help me out with the run to D.C. the other day, could you?" Mac moved closer. "Matter of fact, Gene, I need a little help now. Guess you heard about Tanky?"

Gene staggered back a few steps, slipping in the mud. "Tanky, yeah. Poor sonnavabitch. The cops was here today. Your relation, Jett, as a matter of fact. Hauled me inta the station, but I wasn't no help to them. I don't know nothing. You know who did it?"

"Same guys I delivered the Porsche to. The Mafia. Now they're after me."

Gene backed toward the trailer door. "Look, Mac, somebody might have followed you here. I got a family to look after."

Mac's arm shot out and held the door. He stepped nearer to Gene. "The way I see it, Gene, you owe me. What I need is a 4-wheel drive vehicle and some cash."

"Cash! I ain't got no cash." He measured the look on Mac's face, now inches from his own. "Take my brother-in-law's pickup. It's next door." Gene waved his arm. "I got the key, even. I was supposed to fix his headlight tomorrow. Ain't nothing wrong with the engine."

By the time Mac had pulled off in the old pickup, Gene was already at the phone. "Yessir, Mr. DeMarco, I told your man I'd let you know. He just left in a 1985 Chevy truck— black. I got the license number. Yessir, when you get me the cash. He didn't say where he was headed, but he wanted a 4-wheel drive. No Sir, I done my best. Well, I tried, Mr. De-Marco, but he's a crazy sonnavabitch. I tell ya, if it was me, I'd be getting the hell outta here." When Gene hung up the phone, he yelled to Georgia over the blaring TV, "Done stuck it to that cocky bastard, McCabe. Picked us up a nice piece of change. Whadda think of your ol' man now?" Silently, he added that Georgia didn't need to know it was Mob money. Money was money. Besides, he'd also settled a long-standing score with his brother-in-law. Not a bad night's work.

* * * *

By the time Jett tried to get some sleep, the steady rain had turned into a downpour. Thunder crashed, echoing off the hillsides. He couldn't sleep and started pacing the small rooms. The electric flicked off and on, not as bright as the blue-white flashes of lightning. Tomorrow, he thought, he'd make the rounds of all Mac's old haunts. He'd turn up. Then the phone rang. Checking his watch, Jett realized it was almost midnight.

"Jett," Nate Kincaid's voice sounded hollow through the crackling wire. "Crazy thing. Gene Gray's brother-in-law, lives right next to Gene, just reported that his pickup was stolen in the last hour. He had run out to check whether his shed roof was leaking and saw his pickup was gone. It's a '85 Chevy, black, 4-wheel drive. He suspects Gene. See, Gene had the key." Jett wasn't listening.

"Yeah, thanks, Nate. Listen…" The line went dead. He banged down the phone.

Jett couldn't sleep; he kept trying to put things together. Tonight, Mac had heisted a truck in Great Cacapon. He had to be hiding out somewhere nearby. Even with Mac, there was a limit to how far he could travel on foot in this weather. He wouldn't have been able to take the girl with him. He would have left her in a summer cottage somewhere near where the last one hundred dollar bill was found. So they had to be near Briary Bottom, which was only a few miles from Great Cacapon. If the truck had been stolen between 10:00 and 11:00 o'clock, it was doubtful Mac would have been able to return across the low water bridge—water too high. He'd have taken the mountain road back for the girl and this would slow him down. Nate had said that the stolen vehicle had been a 4-wheel drive, which made sense. That area was pretty rough, isolated country, especially on a night like this, with one storm front rolling in after another.

* * * *

SUNDAY, MAY 8th: Jett couldn't sleep. He had a feeling Rosa would show up for Mass in the morning. Finally, at about 3:00 A.M. he got up and pulled on some jeans and a T-shirt. Rain wasn't drumming loudly on the roof anymore, so why wait for morning and take a chance of missing them? He strapped on his police service holster, with its service issue 9-millimeter automatic, grabbed his jacket, and went out the door. Steering the Bronco down the long, twisting driveway toward the main road, Jett realized just how much damage the storm had done. Tree limbs were down everywhere. The headlights picked up rivers of muddy water racing down the gullies alongside the road. Suddenly, he had to jolt the Bronco to a stop. A huge tree trunk barred the road ahead. "Shit!" Jett shouted as he got out of the truck and slipped in the deep mud.

Bending over, he examined the position of the massive trunk. "Nobody's gonna get by this for a while," he muttered. The blow to the back of his head caught him completely by surprise. Instinctively, he rolled over in the mud and tried to get to his feet, but cold steel pushed into the back of his neck.

"Get up, country boy," a deep voice ordered.

Slightly dazed, Jett struggled to his feet, trying to back away. But a hard, muscled arm grabbed him. Looking at the man, he saw just how big he was—a big, surly hit man in a muddy three-piece suit. "Let go of me, you fatass bastard!"

The grip tightened. "Shuddup. We'd have grabbed you earlier if this tree hadn't blocked the road. Where's Mac and the girl, the Italian girl?"

"Don't know who you're talking about," Jett winced at the pressure on his arm.

"Sure you know, McCabe. That hick kid is related to you. You're probably hiding the two of them. Where?" The voice was close to his ear.

I told you I don't know. I ain't seen that no-good kid in weeks. But look, I can take you to where I think they may be hiding. It's a long shot."

"You better not be messing with me. This shitty weather and these shitty roads have been working on my nerves. Capisci?"

Jett was lockstep marched to a dark-colored Lincoln waiting at the end of the drive. His captor frisked him and grunted with satisfaction when he found the service automatic. "You're a cop, ain't you?" He shoved Jett into the back seat, then climbed in beside him. "Hey, Vince, this guy's a cop, got his service piece."

The man behind the wheel snorted. "So what? Let's get this over with." He gunned the engine and the car shot forward.

"Now, country boy," his surly companion growled, "where to?"

"Turn left on Route 9, toward Great 'Capon." He tried to get a look at the driver. From what he could see, he didn't recognize either hood. He was pretty sure they hadn't been in the "DeMarco family file." Jett wondered if Jimmy DeMarco was bringing in talent from out of town? It was possible. If so, DeMarco really wanted the girl bad. Damn, stupid kids.

"Yeah, 'Great' Cacapon. We been there," Jett's captor snorted. "Great place isn't it, Vince? Gotta be at least two dozen hicks live there and one general store. Great big place, eh?" The driver grunted in reply.

Twenty minutes later, the Lincoln was climbing up the mountain road that led in the back way to Briary Bottom. "Goddamn car's wider than the road," Vince muttered.

As they neared the crest of the hill, Vince cursed, as he had to gear down again. "You better really slow down here," Jett warned. "There's a sheer drop down to the river on the right. See, the storm's washed the posts out. Lose a few cars over this cliff each year—don't find them until winter when the leaves are off the trees."

"Shuddup," the man next to him said.

As the Lincoln labored on, Jett shouted, "Ahead, watch out! Road washed out ahead!" The driver slammed on the brakes, Jett jerked the door open, flung himself out onto the road, and rolled over the side of the cliff.

Hellava stupid thing to do, Jett thought as he hurtled downward through the mud and underbrush. Sharp, jagged rocks gouged at his body and tore at his clothes. Finally, he landed in a thorny briar thicket, bruised, shaken, but alive. It was then that he heard the Lincoln's wheels spinning and the men cursing. He could just make out the headlights far above him. He was damn lucky, he realized, as he dragged himself into a sitting position and checked for serious injuries. Then he pulled himself up and moved off along the side of the mountain. "Dumbass hoods, try to find this country boy now," he shouted.

* * * *

Jett had struggled into Great Cacapon about 5:00 A.M., gotten to a phone and called Nate Kincaid. Nate had picked him up, brought him clothes, and was now driving him to

Berkeley Springs. Rubbing his bruised neck, Jett tried to find a comfortable position in the police car. He ached everywhere. Glancing over at Kincaid, he guessed he'd have to revamp his opinion of old Nate. He hoped they would make it to the Catholic Church on time.

* * * *

Rosie and Mac left the cliff top house early on Sunday morning. The storm had finally worn itself out, but had left destruction in its wake. The old pickup crashed through deep ruts. Clutching the seat, Rosie whispered prayers in Italian. At least twice, they hit washouts.

Mac kept going over his run-in with Gene. He couldn't put his finger on it, but something about Gene had bothered him. Even for a sneaky sonnavabitch, Gene had been more nervous than usual. What had he known that Mac had not?

Glancing over at Rosie, he noted the tightness around her mouth, her wide-eyed stare. The poor girl had been through a lot and never complained. "Don't worry, Rosie. Once we leave Berkeley Springs, we'll be in Martinsburg in about half an hour. Then we'll hit the Interstate and head for Canada."

Instead of showing signs of relief, Rosie started sobbing, "Dio mio, Dio mio, what of the gift?" We won't know where to find the convent in Canada."

"Chrissakes," Mac shouted as the truck plunged into another washout. "Rosie, you need to give as much thought to the living as the dead. I told you I'd help you and I will, but right now we're in a hell of a mess. The Mafia's out there somewhere looking for us."

"I know, Mac, but I can't give up now. The Mafia will never look for us in a church. I will be forever grateful, Mac." She had stopped crying.

Mac's mind raced to at least ten hopeful conclusions, but he said matter-of-factly, "We'll stop at the Catholic church in Berkeley Springs. It's on the way. Will the priest have some kind of book of convents, or something?"

"I don't know. But it's a start." Rosie brightened. "I will ask to speak to the priest. He will know about the convent. It's Sunday. Maybe I can even go to Mass. You see, there is much I must confess…light candles for." She looked down.

Puzzled, Mac didn't see what she could possibly have to confess. Before they pulled onto Route 9, he stopped and switched the license plate. He had kept the plate he'd found at Tanky's garage, figuring it would come in handy. When they pulled up in front of St. Vincent's, it was almost time for early Mass. Mac checked up and down the deserted street. He considered telling Rosie that this was crazy. But she was already getting out of the truck.

The interior of the church was dark and foreboding. The bleeding Christ gazed down accusingly from the crucifix. Mac shifted from one foot to another, then finally sat down in a pew. He had never been at ease in church, and long accustomed feelings of guilt swept over him. Not even the Catholics could match local evangelicals for laying on feelings of guilt and damnation. This was the first time he had even stepped inside a church in the ten years since his mother had died. The banked flowers on the alter brought the funeral back to him. His mother had been buried from a simple Protestant church, which had overflowed with McCabes and their kin. At thirteen, Mac had been abandoned to his alcoholic father. He had known that his life had been changed forever, and this prediction had come true. He had become none of the things his mother had wanted for him. She had been the last person to see any good in him—until he had met Rosie. He watched her now as she lit a candle in front of a statue of the Virgin Mary. He knew he couldn't wipe out the mistakes of the last ten years, but could he start again? God, just being inside a church spooked him. He was beginning to think like a preacher. What he needed was a smoke.

Mac watched a priest enter the area in front of the altar and busy himself at something. He was a stooped, old man and moved slowly. Now the priest's head jerked up and he squinted over his shoulder toward the door. Mac had also heard the door open. He knew that two men had entered. Listening, he knew that one of them was walking with a very slight limp. Although he had expected other worshipers, Mac had been prepared for the hesitant steps of the sinful or the shuffling of the aged, not these decisive footfalls. Continuing to stare straight ahead, he felt the first sparks of apprehension. The old priest froze in the act of pouring wine as he listened to the approaching men. Only Rosie appeared unconcerned as she knelt at the shrine. The student backpack she wore made her look very young and innocent, encircled in the soft glow of the candlelight.

Tensing, Mac realized that the two men had separated, each continuing down a side aisle. The one with the limp slid into a seat behind him and to the right, but the man didn't kneel to pray. Suddenly, the silver cup fell out of the old priest's hands and clattered to the floor. Bright red wine sparkled in puddles around his black robes. Clumsily, the priest started his rituals again. His high, thin voice echoed hollowly through the silent church. Mac had already gauged the distance to the door and to the area behind the altar. He should have never let himself get separated from Rosie. His mind raced. These men were Catholics too. Would they tear up a church when a priest was saying Mass? They could wait; after all, they had time on their side.

The footsteps were so light that at first Mac didn't realize the second man on the far side of the church was moving forward. He cursed himself for a fool; Tanky's gun was hidden in the truck. Straining to listen, Mac knew the second man was advancing, but his steps were now tentative. From the corner of his eye, he saw the man approaching the altar. His powerful hands were folded in prayer. He was big, at least 250 pounds, Mac estimated. Big to walk so softly. The dark suit strained over his hulking frame. A small gold earring and several gold chains caught the candlelight. Easing himself into a kneeling position at the altar rail, he bowed his head. Mac noticed that his pants' cuffs were caked with mud.

"Well, if this don't beat all," Mac muttered to himself. "He's gonna take the bread and wine before he does us in."

Suddenly, the church door was thrown open. Mac turned to see a group of elderly women surging down the aisle toward the altar. They bristled with large pocketbooks and umbrellas, charging like an armed military group. Some were looking for seats; others were bowing their heads and heading toward the altar. Jumping up, he vaulted over the seats in front of him and ran toward Rosie. She looked terrified but grabbed his hand, and together they raced toward the left side of the altar. Frantic screams and the curses of the two men followed them. Finding a door open, they ran down a passageway and through a side door to the street. As they took off in the old black truck, the two hoods erupted out of the of the church door. Mac heard the thunks the bullets made as they drove into the truck bed. "Keep down, Rosie," he yelled. "Keep down!" He turned onto a side street, tires squealing. After all, this was his home ground; he knew where he was going. They could kiss his butt, if they could find him!

* * * *

The old Chevy truck skidded around corners and roared up narrow back streets. In minutes, Rosie and Mac were clear of the town and thundering down country roads. "Can't beat a Chevy," Mac yelled over at Rosie. "Look at this old lady go. Probably the only thing I'll ever have to thank Gene for."

"We could have been killed in there," Rosie whispered.

Mac swerved off onto a dirt road that headed toward the mountain. "Don't worry, Rosie, we're gonna make it now. This is a great shortcut. It'll soon turn into a logging track, but it'll get us over the mountain. We'll come out just a few miles from the Interstate." His eyes glittered a deep blue. The adrenalin was pumping and he felt great. "We've seen the last of them crazy hoods, Rosie. I told you I'd look out for you."

The truck bounced over the rough road, meant to be used by heavy-duty logging equipment in low gear. As the grade increased, the going got tougher. The old Chevy engine coughed and sputtered as the truck strained, crawling upward. No matter, he knew they'd make it. "Look at this view, Rosie. Is this here beautiful, or what?"

Rosie looked down at the sheer drop below, and her eyes rolled. The truck's tires looked to be only inches from the edge. "Dio mio, perfavore," she said softly.

"Don't worry, Rosie, I done this before when I was dead drunk, and in the middle of the night. No problem." Mac glanced down at the rolling blue slopes. This might be the last time he'd ever see this place. "Chrissakes," he whistled between his teeth. It couldn't be, but it was. He saw a blue and tan state police car laboring up the logging road not too far below them. He knew the souped-up engines favored by the troopers. The old Chevy didn't stand a chance. Without hope, he floored the accelerator. How in hell could this have happened? "Jett," he muttered. "He's the only sonnavabitch would think of this shortcut, showed it to me himself. Jett musta gotten hooked up with the State boys. Probably pissed as hell about the stuff we borrowed from his cabin." Rosie didn't answer, but she looked more scared than ever.

* * * *

Jett leaned out the window of the police car, yelling like crazy at the Chevy truck.

"Cool off, they can't hear you," Nate said.

"I'd forgotten all about this road. Only a damn fool would attempt it."

"Yeah, well too bad we missed them at the church. We were only minutes behind them." Nate shifted into a lower gear. "Bet that's the most exciting Mass they ever had at St. Vincent's. A couple of minutes earlier and we'd have grabbed those hoods in the Lincoln."

"Nate, I'm just hoping the APB you put out will haul them in. At least they're not on Mac's tail anymore."

"Well, we sure as hell are. We got them now."

* * * *

Cresting the top of the mountain, the old Chevy truck started rolling downward, bouncing off fallen rocks and debris. "Whoa," Mac shouted. "Maybe we can outrun them suckers. Just need a little luck."

"Yes, you can do it, Mac." Rosie was calm now. "It's better to have the American police chase us than the Mafia."

The Chevy truck rounded a hairpin turn and lady luck rushed up to meet them in the form of a gully-sized washout in the middle of the road. Mac floored the gas pedal. The old truck took off and actually sailed across, landing with a grinding jolt on the other side, but still moving.

"We done it, Rosie, we done it!" Mac grabbed her arm and pulled her close. His left arm steadied the steering wheel around the turns. "Keep checking out the rear window and let me know when them dumbass cops land in that washout. No way they're gonna make it across."

A few minutes later, the crash of metal and roar of the police car's engine told the story. "We done it, Baby. We're on our way to Canada!" Mac and Rosie were both hollering their heads off.

The Chevy truck bumped and jolted its way down the mountain, finally running into a secondary road that intersected the Interstate. They weren't followed.

* * * *

The police radio crackled with an unintelligible reply. "I told you, get a car up here on the double," Nate yelled. "Yeah, send a four-wheel drive. And be sure you get the description of the Chevy truck out right away. Check on the Interstate. That's where they're headed." He slammed down the receiver.

* * * *

Barreling up the Interstate, Rosie and Mac were jubilant. She was still sitting close to him, and every so often Mac would give her hand a squeeze and lean down to kiss her hair.

When the dark Lincoln passed them, it must have been traveling at least one hundred miles an hour. Now the Lincoln had slowed down and was holding up the heavy traffic. It changed lanes and swerved in behind them, hugging the truck's bumper.

"Will you look at that," Mac said. "It's the same two guys. They're trying to force us to the side of the road. How in the hell did they find us?" Seeing his chance, he switched to the left lane and jolted over the median strip to the southbound lanes. The Lincoln was held up in traffic and couldn't follow. In a couple of miles, Mac crossed the median again. Heading north, he spotted a Rest Stop sign and turned into the parking area. Time to pick up another vehicle, and what better place? He cut over the landscaped grounds to the back of the facility. Leaving the truck under cover of trees, Rosie and Mac dragged their gear toward the group of buildings.

* * * *

The West Virginia State Police car slowed as it approached a dark Lincoln sedan pulled over on the shoulder of Northbound I-81. Location, a mile south of the Rest Stop. It matched the description on a recently posted APB. Reading out the license plate number over the radio, the trooper got a negative. But still, what was the car doing there? There were two men in the front, one talking into a cell phone. The police car continued up the Interstate. In a few miles this would be Maryland's problem, the trooper rationalized.

* * * *

"Try to change the way you look," Mac told Rosie as they parted at the Rest Stop's main building. "Meet me by the picnic tables quick as you can." Rosie nodded and disappeared into the Women's Restroom.

In the Men's Restroom, Mac searched through his gear for a razor. Quickly, he shaved off the short beard that Rosie had liked so well. He emerged having added a jacket, a bush hat he'd found in the truck, and sunglasses to his outfit. Moving through the weekend crowd, he looked for Rosie.

Surrounding the picnic tables, a large family group was celebrating. Mac edged closer. A heavy man with dark curling hair and beard held up a cake glowing with three candles. The whole gang was singing, bellowing away in some foreign language. The object of all this attention, a small blond girl, sat on the bearded man's lap and clapped her hands to the song. It finished with a rousing, "Bravo, Renee."

The man stood up. Balancing the cake in one arm and the little girl in the other, he started a slow, lumbering dance around the tables, accompanied by the rhythmic clapping and cheers of his audience. Mac was surprised at how short, but muscular he was. His bull neck ended with a ruff of black, furry hair at his shirt collar. His chest was square as a block of concrete in the flowered Hawaiian shirt. Moving slowly around the clapping onlookers, he finally came to a halt in front of a heavyset blond woman and Rosie. Was it Rosie? She had tied her hair back in a bandanna and had changed her clothes. Wait. Mac looked more closely. This girl was pregnant. A large, round mound swelled under his old plaid shirt. A small gold chain with a medallion dangled from her hand. She held it out to the child. More cheers and excited discussion followed. Just then, Rosie saw Mac and beckoned to him.

Mac hesitated, but from the corner of his eye, he caught sight of a dark Lincoln entering the parking area. Through the tinted glass, he made out two men in the front. One was very large. By now, Mac was already moving toward the crowd at the picnic tables. Smiling, he joined Rosie.

Taking his hand, Rosie introduced him first to the couple with the little girl, then to the others. He couldn't understand a word of it, but smiled, nodded, and shook hands. Suddenly, she reached up and kissed him. The group responded with cheers of "Felicitations!"

"They're French Canadians, going home to Montreal," Rosie whispered. "I told them we were running away to get married—that my family don't approve and may follow us. And our truck just broke down here at the Rest Stop."

Mac stared at her, amazed. "Great story," he told her. "Do you think we can hitch a ride with them? Because your 'family' is already here, in the parking lot."

Rosie stiffened, but didn't look around and kept smiling. She went over to the short, barrel-chested man she had called Louie. Trying to stay in the center of the group, Mac helped the women pack up the picnic baskets. They smiled at him, giggling and whispering in French to each other. Glancing around, Mac couldn't pick out the Mafia soldiers, but he knew they were there. Now he knew how a trapped animal felt while he waited for the hunter. He was sure that he could probably get away if he bolted now and left Rosie to take her chances. But no, if he had been going to cut out, he would have done it a long time ago. If nothing else, he'd promised to get her to that convent, although this whole gift thing mystified him.

Rosie returned and pulled him aside. "They'll take us over the border...all the way to Montreal if we want. They're on their way home from Florida, so they're driving straight through."

Relief showed on Mac's face. He asked, "What about the border?"

"Louie said not to worry, to keep quiet and leave it all to him. He likes us." She grabbed Mac's hand. "They all like us. We have a romance story, yes?"

Over the top of Rosie's head, Mac spotted a man walking with a slight limp. He seemed to be searching the grounds. Quickly, he turned his head and pulled Rosie toward the center of the group. "Ask them if we can help load up. We gotta get outta here fast."

In ten minutes Mac and Louie had shoved the last of the coolers and baskets into the back of a large panel van. Rosie and Mac climbed in and found places to sit among the luggage. Before closing the door, Louie grinned at them and said, "Demain matin, Montreal." Rosie translated, "Tomorrow morning we'll be in Montreal."

A white Tarus station wagon and a Ford Explorer made up the rest of the French Canadian caravan. As they pulled out and headed north up the Interstate, Mac caught sight of the limping gangster and his hulking, fatass pal standing by the Lincoln. They looked puzzled and mad as hell. Mac grinned and nudged Rosie. "Idioti," she sneered and made an Italian style hand sign.

Mac started to laugh. Soon they were both howling with laughter. "Don't seem like a very nun-like way to act," Mac said. She shrugged and moved closer to him. Putting an arm around her, he continued, "But you can act any way you want as far as I'm concerned. I gotta hand it to you, Rosie. You got us outta this one."

"It wasn't really me. When I was in the Women's Restroom changing my clothes, I found a chain with a medal of St. Ursula. I asked around outside and found out it belonged to Louie's wife. It was the little girl's birthday gift. I just returned it and they were very grateful. But Mac, now I'm sure we'll make it to the convent. This was a sign from St. Ursula herself."

"Yeah, the convent. Well, they gotta have convents in Canada. These Frenchies should know." He shot her a puzzled look. "Do they all think you're pregnant?"

"Not now. After Louie agreed to take us, I told him I was just trying to disguise the way I looked. Louie laughed." Rosie reached under the plaid shirt and pulled out the old student backpack. "This was the bambino." She grinned. "Of course, just to be sure Louie wouldn't say no, I offered to pay him."

"Pay him? With what?"

Opening the backpack, Rosie pulled out stacks of one hundred dollar bills, held together with rubber bands. "Uncle Vito's gift to the Ursuline Convent."

"You're kidding. You've had this all along?" Mac inspected the stacks of bills. He was shocked and just a little angry. Things would sure have been a lot easier if he'd had this money. He glanced at her. Didn't she trust him? Should she? He started to laugh again. "You're one hellava woman, Rosie. One surprise after another. How'd you get all this money?"

"Well, back at Uncle Vito's garage." She looked serious now and a little scared. "You remember I told you that he and I were in the storage room counting things. When he saw the Mafia car drive up, he got very upset and went to a secret place in the little room. He came back and handed me a box. He said if anything happened to him, it was mine. Never to forget to pray for him. Then he told me to run and hide. Later, when I knew he was dead, I did what he said. I took my lunch and book out of my backpack, and just shoved the stacks of bills in there. I knew the only way I could take this money was to give it to the Sisters. They would pray for Uncle Vito's soul. It was all I could do for him."

Looking relieved, she smiled that slow, beautiful smile of hers. Then she leaned over and kissed him, a real kiss this time—a long, lingering kiss. "Here, Mac," she handed him a stack of hundreds. "This is for you, Uncle Vito's gift. He would agree you've earned it. It can take you far in Canada, or it can be his wedding gift to us. You have to decide.

ABOUT THE AUTHOR

Sally Walker Brinkmann was born in Washington, D.C. She attended George Washington University and graduated from Shepherd College with a BA in English. She worked eight years as writer and editor of *The Sandpiper*, an employee newspaper of U.S. Silica Corporation, a mining operation in Berkeley Springs, West Virginia. She also taught English in West Virginia for seventeen years.

Several of her shorter stories have been published in local anthologies. Four of her plays have been produced by the Morgan Arts Council Theater Project. She has won awards in the West Virginia Writers' annual competitions for both drama and fiction.

Her first novel, *Rebel Traveler*, appeared to acclaim in 2013. Her second novel, *Between River and Mountain*, a Civil War story set in Morgan County, is due to be published by Wildside Press in late 2014.

Much of her writing is about survival, as it's always been an issue in the hill country. The unique local dialect and rhythm of speech are part of her writing.

Made in the USA
Charleston, SC
22 October 2014